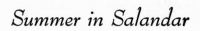

Summer in Salandar

By H. E. Bates

H. E. BATES

Summer
in Salandar

An Atlantic Monthly Press Book
Little, Brown and Company • *Boston* • *Toronto*

ATLANTIC–LITTLE, BROWN BOOKS
ARE PUBLISHED BY
LITTLE, BROWN AND COMPANY
IN ASSOCIATION WITH
THE ATLANTIC MONTHLY PRESS

Contents

Death of a Huntsman

1

EVERY weekday evening, watches ready, black umbrellas neatly rolled and put away with neat black Homburgs on carriage racks, attaché cases laid aside, newspapers poised, the fellow travelers of Harry Barnfield, the city gentlemen, waited for him to catch — or rather miss — the five-ten train.

As the last minutes jerked away on the big station clock above wreaths of smoke and steam the city gentlemen sat with jocular expectation on the edges of carriage seats or actually craning necks from carriage windows, as if ready to check with stop watches the end of Harry Barnfield's race with time.

"Running it pretty fine tonight."

"Doomed. Never make it."

"Oh! Trust Harry."

"Absolutely doomed. Never make it."

"Oh! Harry'll make it. Trust Harry. Never fluked it yet. Trust Harry."

All Harry Barnfield's friends, like himself, lived in the country, kept farms at a heavy loss and came to London for business every day. J. B. (Punch) Warburton, who was in shipping and every other day or so brought up from his farm little perforated boxes of fresh eggs for less fortunate friends in the city, would get ready, in mockery, to hold open the carriage door.

"Action stations." J. B. Warburton, a wit, was not called Punch for nothing. "Grappling hooks at ready!"

"This is a bit of bad. Dammit, I believe —" George Reed Thompson also had a farm. Its chief object, apart from losing money, was to enable him to stock a large Deepfreeze, every summer, with excellent asparagus, strawberries, raspberries, spring chickens, pheasant, partridges, and vegetables, all home-raised. "Harry's going to let us down — !"

"Nine-ten, nine-fifteen." Craning from the window, Freddie Jekyll, who was a stockbroker and rode, every spring, with great success at local point-to-points, would actually begin to check off the seconds. "Nine-twenty —"

"Officer of the watch, keep a sharp lookout there!"

"Aye, aye, sir."

"All ashore who are going ashore."

"Aye, aye, sir."

"A firm hold on those grappling hooks!"

"Dammit, he's missed it. I make it eleven past already."

Sometimes a whistle would blow; sometimes a final door would slam with doom along the far hissing reaches of the waiting express. But always, at last, without fail, the city gentlemen would be able to raise, at first severally and then collectively, a joyful, bantering cheer.

"Here, Harry, here! Here, old boy!"

Cheering, signaling frantically from windows, thrusting out of them Malacca handles of umbrellas as if they were really grappling hooks, they would drag Harry Barnfield finally aboard.

"Five-nine point twelve," they would tell him. "New world record."

Panting, smiling modestly from behind sweat-clouded spectacles, Harry Barnfield would lean shyly on the handle of his umbrella, struggling to recover breath. Laughing, the city gentlemen would begin to unfold their papers, offering congratulations.

"Well run, Harry. Damn near thing though, old boy. Thought you were doomed."

But that, they always told themselves, was the great thing about Harry. You could always rely on Harry. You could always be sure of Harry. Harry would never let you down.

What a good sport he was, they all said, Harry Barn-

field. There were no two ways, no possible arguments
about that. There was no shadow of harm in Harry Barnfield.

2

ALL HIS LIFE Harry Barnfield, who looked ten years more
middle-aged than forty-three, had been fond of horses
without ever being a good rider of them.

His body was short and chunky. It had the odd appearance, especially when he rode a horse, of having had a middle cut of six or seven inches removed from between ribs
and groin, leaving the trunk too short between legs and
shoulders. It was also rather soft, almost pulpy, as if his
bones had never matured. This pulpiness was still more
noticeable in the eyes, which behind their spectacles
were shy, gray, protuberant and rather jellified, looking altogether too large for his balding head.

All this gave him, in the saddle, a floppy, overeager
air and, as the black tails of his coat flew out behind, the
look of a fat little bird trying hard to fly from the ground
and never quite succeeding. Riding, he would tell you,
was awful fun, and his voice was high and squeaky.

Every evening, ten minutes before the arrival of the
train that brought him back to the country with his
friends the city gentlemen, he started to give a final polish
to his spectacles, the lenses of which were rather thick. For

five minutes or so he polished them with scrupulous short-
sightedness on a square of cream silk that he kept in his
breast pocket, huffing on them with brief panting little
breaths, showing a pink, lapping tongue.

The effect of this scrupulous preparation of the spectacles was to make his face seem quite absurdly alight. Smiling from behind the glittering lenses, calling good night to
his friends, he came out of the station with wonderful
eagerness, head well in front of the chunky body, black
umbrella prodding him forward, attaché case paddling the
air from the other hand, bowler hat tilted slightly back-
ward and sitting on the loose crimson ears.

Once out of the station he sucked in a long deep breath
— as if to say: ah, at last, the country! The short little
body seemed transformed with eager exhilaration. Fields
came down almost to within reach of the fences surrounding the station coalyards and on late spring evenings the
greening hedges were brilliant and thick as banks of pars-
ley. Primroses and sprays of pale mauve lady's-smocks
sprang lushly from damp dykes below the hedgerows and
along the roads beyond these were black-boughed cherry
orchards in white thick bloom. A few weeks later apple
orchards and great snow mounds of hawthorn came into
blossom and in the scent of them he could taste the first
milkiness of summer just as surely as he tasted winter in
the first sweet-acid tang of the big-toothed Spanish
chestnut leaves as they began to swim down from the trees

in November, haunting the dark staves of baring copses.

Then, as he drove home in his car, much of his eagerness vanished. He gradually took on the air of being calm
and free: free of the dusty odors of city offices, city ter-
mini, free of his friends the city gentlemen in the smoky
train. His body relapsed completely into quietness. His
big eyes stopped their agitation and became, behind the
bulging lenses of the spectacles, perfectly, blissfully at
rest.

It took him twenty minutes to drive out to the big dou-
ble-gabled house of old red brick that had, behind it, a
row of excellent stables with a long hayloft above. He had
been awfully lucky, he would tell you, to get the house. It
was absolutely what he wanted. The stables themselves
were perfect and at the front were four good meadows, all
flat, bordered by a pleasant alder-shaded stream.

The fields were about twenty acres in all, and from
three of them, in June, he gathered all the hay he would
need. Then in early autumn he took down part of the
fences and put up a run of four brushwood jumps and
over these, on Saturdays and Sundays, he started prac-
ticing jumping. Sometimes, too, in the same inelastic way
that never improved during the entire hunting season, he
practiced jumping the brook. Then by late November the
alders lost the last of their leaves; the hazels, the willows
and the sweet chestnuts became naked too and presently
he could feel the sting of frost in his nostrils as he brought

his horse in through the blue-gray twilights across which the sound of croaking pheasants settling to roost clattered like wintry frightened laughter.

"That you, Harry? I hope to God you didn't forget the gin?"

"Yes, it's me, Katey."

If it had not been that he was almost always blinking very slightly, with a sort of mechanical twitch, behind the glasses, it might have seemed that he had never lost the habit of surprise as his wife called to him, her voice somewhere between a croak and a cough, from the kitchen.

It might also have seemed, from the snap in her voice, that she was not very tolerant of forgetfulness. But fortunately neither surprise nor forgetfulness were habits of his. He was never surprised and he never forgot the gin.

"On the hall table, Katey," he would tell her. "Any message from Lewis? I'm just hopping across the yard."

His inquiry about Lewis, his groom, was never answered, except by another cough, and this never surprised him either. His only real thought was for his horses. In summer he had only to whistle and they came to him from across the meadows. In winter he walked quietly across the courtyard to the stables, let himself in, touched for a moment the warm flanks of the two animals, said good night to them exactly as if they were children and then, almost on tiptoe, let himself out again. Outside, if there were stars, he generally stopped to look up at them, breathing over again the good country air. Then he stiffened, braced his short pulpy body and went back into the house again.

"Where the hell did you say the gin was? Every bloody evening you slink off like a badger and I'm left wondering where you dump the stuff."

"I told you where it was, Katey." From the hall table he would quietly pick up the gin bottle and take it to the kitchen. "Here. Here it is."

"Then why the hell couldn't you say so?"

"I did say so."

"You talk like a squeak-mouse all the time. How do you expect me to hear if you talk like a damn squeak-mouse?"

His wife was tallish, fair and very blowzy. She looked, he always thought, remarkably like some caged and battered lioness. Her hair, which she wore down on her shoulders, had passed through several stages of blondness. Sometimes it was almost white, bleached to lifelessness; sometimes it was the yellow of a ferret and he would not have been surprised, then, to see that her eyes were pink; sometimes it was like coarse rope, with a cord of darker hair twisting through the center. But the most common effect was that of the lioness, restless, caged and needing a comb.

"Any news, Katey?" he would say. "Anything been happening?"

"Where, what and to whom?" she would ask him. "To bloody whom? Tell me." The fingers of both hands were stained yellow with much smoking. Her lips were rather thick. She had also mastered the art of getting a cigarette to stick to the lower, thicker one without letting it fall into whatever she was cooking. She was very fond of cooking. The air, every evening, was full of odors of herbs, garlic, wine vinegars and frying onions. The smell of frying onions invariably made him ravenously hungry but it was always nine o'clock, sometimes ten, occasionally still later, before she would yell across the hall to where he sat sipping sherry in the drawing room:

"Come and get it if you want it. And if you don't want it —" the rest of the sentence asphyxiated in coughing.

Sometimes, so late at night, he did not want it. Excellent though the food often was, he found himself not hungry any more. He sat inelastically at table, ate with his fork and sipped a glass of claret, perhaps two. She, on the other hand, more than ever like the lioness, ravenous far beyond feeding time, ate eyelessly, no longer seeing the food, the table or himself through mists of gin.

"Forgot to tell you — Lewis saw that kid riding through the place again today. Rode clean through the courtyard, by the cucumber house and out the other side."

"Good heavens, didn't Lewis choke her off?"

"Gave her hell he says."

"And what happened? What did she say?"

"Said she'd been told it was perfectly all right. You'd never mind."

"But good grief," he said, "we can't have that. We can't have strangers riding through the place as if it's their own. That won't do. That simply won't do —"

"All right," she said. "All right. You tell her. I've told her. Lewis has told her. Now you tell her. It's your turn."

She lit a cigarette, pushed more food into her mouth and began laughing. A little stream of bright crimson tomato sauce ran down her chin. A shred or two of tobacco clung to her front teeth and there was actually a touch of pink, the first bloodshot vein or two, in the whites of her eyes.

"But who *is* she?"

"Search me. *You* find out. It's *your* turn —"

Open-mouthed, she laughed again across the table, the cigarette dangling this time from the lower lip as she mockingly pointed her glass at his face.

He knew that this gesture of fresh derision meant that she no longer saw him very well. Already the eyes had begun their swimming unfocused dilations.

"All right," he said. "I'll speak to her."

"Good," she said. "That's the brave Harry. Brave old Harry."

As she threw back her head, laughing openly now, letting the cigarette fall into her plate of half-eaten food, revealing relics of her last mouthful smeared across her lips and her tongue, he did not ask himself why he had ever married her. It was too late for asking that kind of question.

"When does she appear?" he said.

"Oh, off and on. Any time. On and off —"

"I'll try to catch her on Saturday," he said. "Or Sunday."

Derisively and deliberately she raised her hand, not laughing now, in a sort of mock benediction.

"Now don't be rash, Harry dear. Brave old Harry," she said. "Don't be rash. She might catch you."

3

ON THE FOLLOWING Sunday morning, as he walked up past the cucumber house to where a path led through two wicket gates to the meadows beyond, a light breeze was coming off the little river, bringing with it the scent of a few late swaths of hay. The glass of the cucumber house, with its dark green undertracery of leaves, flashed white in the sun. The summer had been more stormy than fine, with weeks of August rain, and now, in mid-September, the fields were flush with grasses.

He stopped to look inside the cucumber house. Under the glass the temperature had already risen to ninety-five. Thick green vines dripped with steamy moisture. Columns of cucumbers, dark and straight, hung down from dense masses of leaves that shut out the strong morning sun.

The cucumbers were his wife's idea. She was very imaginative, he had to admit, about cucumbers. Whereas the average person merely sliced up cucumbers, made them into sandwiches or simply ate them with fresh salmon for lunch in summer, his wife was acquainted with numerous recipes in which cucumbers were cooked, stuffed like *aubergines* or served with piquant sauces or high flavors such as Provençal. Harry Barnfield did not care much for cucumbers. More often than not, cooked or uncooked, they gave him wind, heartburn or chronic indigestion. But over the years of his married life he had learned to eat them because he was too good-natured to deny his wife the chance of surprising guests with dishes they had never heard of before. He well understood her cucumbers and her little gastronomic triumphs with them.

That Sunday morning, as he stood under the steaming shadowy vines, he thought he saw, suddenly, a bright yellow break of sunlight travel the entire length of the glasshouse outside. The leaves of the cucumbers were so thick that it was some moments before he grasped that this was, in fact, a person riding past him on a horse.

Even then, as he discovered when he rushed out of the cucumber house, he was partly mistaken. The horse was merely a pony, blackish brown in color, with a loose black tail.

With impatience he started to shout after it: "Hi! You there! Where do you think you're going? Don't you know — ?" and then stopped, seeing in fact that its rider was nothing more than a young girl in a yellow sweater, jodhpurs, black velvet cap and pigtails. The pigtails too looked black and they hung long and straight down the yellow shoulders, tied at the ends not with ribbon but with short lengths of crimson cord.

The girl did not stop. He started to shout again and then, quite without thinking, began to run after her. "Young lady!" he called. "Young lady! One moment, young lady, one moment please —"

It was thirty or forty yards farther on before he caught up with her. By that time she had stopped, bent down and was already lifting the catch of the first of the wicket gates with the handle of her riding crop.

"Just a moment, young lady, just one moment —"

As he stopped he found himself short of breath and panting slightly. She turned very slightly in the saddle to look at him. Her eyes were brown, motionless and unusually round and large. They seemed, like his own, rather too big for her face.

"Aren't you aware," he said, "that this is private property — this path? It's private property!"

She did not move. She looked, he thought, fifteen, perhaps sixteen, not more than that, though rather well developed for her age. The sleeves of the yellow jumper were half rolled up, showing firm brown forearms that glistened with downy golden hairs. Her face was the same golden brown color, the lips without make-up, so that they too had a touch of brown.

"You really can't ride through here like this," he said. "You've been told before. You really can't, you know."

Again she did not move. He did not know if the large motionless eyes were utterly insolent or merely transfixed in frightened innocence and he was still trying to make up his mind about it when he noticed how straight but relaxed she sat on the pony. He had to admit, even in vexation, that she sat very well; very well indeed, he thought.

"It's very tiresome," he said, "all this. You simply can't ride roughshod over other people's property like this."

"Roughshod?"

Her voice surprised him very much by its deepness. It almost seemed, he thought, like the voice of a woman twice her age.

"Do you really think," she said, "I'm riding roughshod?"

The eyes, still holding him in enormous circles of inquiring innocence, disarmed him with sheer brightness.

"That's neither here nor there," he said. "The simple fact is that you cannot ride when and how you please over other people's property."

"I was told I could."

"Told? By whom?"

"My mother."

At this moment his spectacles began to mist over. For the next second or two she seemed to melt away and become lost to him.

Uneasily he thought to himself that he ought to take his spectacles off, polish them and put them back again. He began to feel inexplicably nervous about this and his hands groped about his face. Then when he realized that if he took off his spectacles he would, with his weak, shortsighted eyes, be able to see her even less well he made the unfortunate compromise of trying to look over the top of them.

She smiled.

"Your mother?" he said. "What has your mother to do with it? Do you mean I know your mother?"

"You *knew* her."

"Oh! And when, pray, would that be?"

He hadn't the slightest idea why he should ask that question and in fact she ignored it completely.

"My name is Valerie Whittington."

"Oh, yes. I see. Oh, yes," he said slowly. "Oh, yes." He was so intensely surprised that, without thinking, he

at once took off his spectacles and rubbed the lenses on
his coat sleeve.

"Is the colonel — ?"

"He died last year."

Again he polished the lenses of the spectacles quickly
on the coat sleeve.

"We've taken the gamekeeper's cottage at Fir Top. I
don't suppose you know it," she said.

"Oh, yes!"

Something made him keep the spectacles in his hand a
little longer.

"I can ride down through the park and along by the
river and then back through the woods across the hill,"
the girl said. "It's a complete circle if I take the path
through here. If not I have to go back the same way again
and you know how it is. It's never so nice going back the
same way."

He murmured something about no, it was never so nice
and then put on his spectacles. Clear, fresh and with that
remarkable blend of insolence and innocent charm, she
stared down at him, making him feel a baffled, fumbling
idiot.

"So it was your mother told you about the path?"

"She just said she was sure you wouldn't mind."

Why, he wondered, did she say that?

"She said you were the sort of man who never did
mind."

Again he felt baffled and stupid.

Then, for the first time, the pony moved. Up to that moment it had kept remarkably still and it was in fact so quiet, standing erect in the hot September sun, that he had been almost unaware that it was there until now, suddenly, it reared its head and shuddered.

Instinctively he put one hand on its flank to calm it down. It quietened almost immediately and she said:

"I'm afraid he's really not big enough for me. But he's the best we can afford for the time."

She ran her hand down the pony's neck, leaning forward as she did so. He saw the muscles of the neck light up like watered silk. At the same time he saw the flanks of the girl tauten, smooth out and then relax again.

"Does your mother ride now?" he said.

"No," she said. "Not now."

"She used to ride very well."

"Yes. She said you'd remember."

Again he felt baffled; again he groped towards his spectacles.

"Well," she said. "I suppose I must go back."

She started to turn the pony round. He found all his many uncertainties stiffen into astonishment.

"I thought you wanted to go on?" he said. "Over the hill?"

"You said you didn't want me to."

"Oh, yes, I know, but that was — I admit — oh, no —

well, I mean —" He found himself incapable of forming a coherent sentence. "By all means — it was simply that I didn't want — well, you know, strangers —"

"I ought to have come and asked you," she said. "I know now. But you were never at home."

"Oh, no, no, no," he said. "Oh, no!"

The pony was still facing the cucumber house, uneasy now. Sunlight was catching the angle of the roof panes, flashing white glare into the animal's eyes in spite of the blinkers, and Harry Barnfield put his hand on its nose, steadying it down.

"I'll be putting up jumps next week," he said. "In the meadows there." The touch of the animal brought back a little, but only a little, of his assurance. "You could — well, I mean if you cared — you could use them. I'm never here weekdays."

She smiled as if to begin to thank him but a flash of light from the cucumber house once again caught the pony's eye, making it rear.

"You'd better turn him round," he said, "and take him along. It's the sun on the cucumber house."

"I will," she said.

He moved forward to unlatch the gate for her. The pony also moved forward. A new wave of uncertainty ran through Harry Barnfield and he said:

"Remember me to your mother, will you? If she would care — Oh! I don't suppose she would like a cucumber?

We have masses. We have too many cucumbers by far."

"We neither of us care for them," she said, "but I'll tell her all the same."

She rode through the gate. He shut the gate after her, leaned on it and watched her ride, at a walk, up the path. After forty or fifty yards the path began to go uphill to where, against the skyline, clumps of pine grew from browning bracken hillocks before the true woods began. The morning was so clear that he could see on the tips of these pines the stiff fresh crusts of the light olive summer cones. He could see also the brown arms of the girl below the rolled sleeves of the yellow sweater, the flecks of white on the short legs of the pony and the knots of red on the pigtails.

He was suddenly aware that there was something disturbing about her without being able to say what it was. In that insolent innocent way of hers she rode very well, he thought, but the pony was quite ridiculous. Her body and the pony simply did not fit each other, any more than her body and her voice seemed part of the same person.

"Edna should get her a horse," he said aloud and then, with sweat breaking out again from under his misty spectacles, began to walk back to the cucumber house.

There he was overcome by embarrassment at remembering how he had been stupid enough to offer the girl a cucumber; and in remembering it forgot completely that he had called her mother by name.

4

SOON AFTER THAT he began to come home on late September evenings to a recurrence of mild gin-dry quips from Katey. He did not really mind being quipped; the city gentlemen made him used to that sort of thing.

"Your girl friend was jumping again today. Here most of the morning and back again before I'd swallowed lunch. Stayed till five. I'd have offered her a bed but I wasn't tight enough."

"I wish you wouldn't call her my girl friend."

"Best I can think of, Harry. You put her up to this game."

Presently she began to use his jumps not only on weekdays but on Saturdays and Sundays too. Sometimes he would wake as early as eight o'clock, look out across the meadows and see the yellow sweater dipping between the barriers of brushwood.

He saw it also as it faded in the twilights. And always he was baffled by the ridiculous nature of the pony, the pigtails and the long impossibly dangling legs of the girl as she rode.

"Your girl friend certainly works at it. Lewis tells me she was here at six the other morning. He was mad. The animal kicked up his mushrooms."

"I do wish you wouldn't call her my girl friend. She's fifteen. Sixteen if she's that."

"From the day they're born," Katey said, "they're women. Never mind their age."

At first he found it an embarrassment, slight but uneasy, to join her at the jumps. He supposed it arose from the fact that in his inelastic way he often fell off the horse. That did not matter very much when he jumped alone but it was awkward, even painful, when people were watching.

In this way he began to ride more cautiously, more dumpily, more stiffly than before. For two week ends he did not jump at all. At the third he heard a clatter of pony hoofs on the stable yard, looked up to see her long legs astride the pony and heard her deep voice say:

"I thought you must be ill, Mr. Barnfield, because you weren't jumping. Mother sent me to inquire."

Her voice, deeper than ever, he thought, startled and disturbed him; and he fumbled for words.

"Oh, no! Oh, no! Perfectly all right, thank you. Oh, no! It's just that the countryside has been looking so lovely that I've been giving the jumps a miss and riding up on the hill instead. In fact I'm just going up there now."

"Do you mind if I ride that way with you?" she said.

Some minutes later they were riding together up the

hillside, under clumps of pines, along paths by which huge bracken fronds were already tipped with fox brown. Late blackberries shone pulpy and dark with bloom in the morning sunlight and where the bracken cleared there ran rose-bright stains of heather, with snow tufts of cotton grass in seed.

"You can smell that wonderful, wonderful scent of pines," she said.

He lifted his face instinctively to breathe the scent of pines and instead was distracted, for it might have been the fiftieth time, by her incongruous legs scratching the lowest tips of bracken fronds as she rode.

"My wife and I were having a slight argument as to how old you were," he said. "Of course it's rude to guess a lady's age but —"

"Oh! I'm ancient," she said. "Positively and absolutely ancient."

He started to smile.

"And how old," she said, "did you say?"

"Oh! Fifteen," he said at once, not really thinking at all. "Perhaps I'll give you sixteen."

"Give me sixteen," she said. "And then seventeen. And then eighteen. And then if you like —"

She stopped. Looking up from the pony she turned on him the enormous circular eyes that appeared so often to be full of naïve insolence and then waited for him, as it were, to recover his breath.

"And then nineteen. And then if you like, next month, you can come to my twentieth birthday."

He was too staggered to bring to this situation anything but absolute silence as they rode to the hilltop.

"I think you're surprised," she said.

"Oh, no! Oh, no!" he said. "Well, yes and no, in a way —"

"Don't you think I look twenty?"

"Well, it's not always absolutely easy —"

"How do you demonstrate age?" she said and he rode to the crest of the hilltop without an answer, his head sweating under his close tweed cap, his spectacles misting and turning to a premature fog-bound landscape the entire valley of morning brilliance below.

He was temporarily saved from making a complete and disastrous fool of himself by hearing the pony breathing hard, in partial distress.

"I think you should give him a blow," he said. "It's a pretty long drag up here."

She thought so too and they both began dismounting. Then, as she swung to the ground, he had a second surprise.

This, he suddenly realized, was the first time he had actually seen her when not on the pony. Standing there, at his own level, she seemed to enlarge and straighten up. He was aware of a pair of splendid yellow shoulders. Riding had made her straight in the back, throwing her breasts well forward, keeping her head erect and high. She was also, he now discovered with fresh uneasiness, slightly taller than he was.

He turned away to tie his horse to a pine. When he had finished he looked round to see her walking, with surprisingly delicate strides for so tall a girl, towards the ridge of the hillside.

Finally she stopped, turned and waved to him. For a single moment he thought she had in her hand a flower of some kind and it looked, he thought, like a scarlet poppy. Then he saw that it was one of the cords she had snatched from her pigtails.

"Come over and look at the view," she called.

By the time he joined her she was sitting down in a patch of bracken. He sat down too: looking, not at the view below him, the map of copse and pasture and hedge-row flecked already with the occasional pure bright chrome of elm and hornbeam, the dense oaks and grass still green as summer, but at the sight of the girl now un-plaiting and combing out the mass of bright brown hair into a single tail.

"You look surprised," she said, "but then I notice you always do."

She started to let her hair fall loosely over her shoulders, until it half enclosed her face. Then she put her hand in the pocket of her jodhpurs and pulled out a powder compact, a lipstick and lastly a small oval mirror with a blue enamel back.

"Do you mind holding that?" she said.

He held the mirror in front of her face. Once or twice she stretched forward, touching his hand, and moved the mirror to one side or the other.

In silence, for perhaps the next five minutes or so, he watched her make up her face. He saw the lips, freed of their dull brownness, thicken, becoming very full, almost overfull, in redness. He saw her smooth with the powder-pad the skin of her face, giving it a tone of milky brown.

Finally she threw back her hair from her shoulders and he had time to notice that the enlargement of the lips, so bright now and almost pouting, had the effect of bringing into proportion the large brown eyes.

"How do I look?" she said.

His immediate impression was that the make-up, the loosened hair and the fuller, brighter lips had softened her completely. It was very like the effect on parched grass of warm and heavy rain.

At the same time he could not help feeling desperately, awkwardly and embarrassingly sorry for her.

"Now do I look twenty?" she said.

It was on the tip of his tongue to say "More — older" and afterwards he knew that it would have pleased her very much if he had, but he said instead:

"What made you do that just now — just here?"

"Oh, God!" she said and the sepulchral wretched cry of her deep voice shocked him so much that his mouth fell open. "I'm so miserable — Oh, God! I can't tell you how miserable I am."

She turned suddenly and, not actually sobbing but with a harsh choke or two, lay face downwards in the bracken, beating her hands on the ground.

Pained and discomforted, he started to move towards her. She seemed to sense the movement and half leaped up.

"Don't touch me!" she howled.

It was the furthest thing from his mind. He stood for a moment with his mouth open and then started blunderingly to walk away.

"Where are you going?" she moaned.

At that second sepulchral cry he stopped.

"I thought you'd rather have it out by yourself."

"I don't want to have it out!" she said. "I don't want to have it out! I don't want to have it out!"

It was beyond him to understand and he wished unhappily that he were back home, jumping or talking to Lewis or having a glass of sherry with Bill Chalmers, his neighbor, or with Punch Warburton, who sometimes came over and talked horses and weather and general gossip before Sunday lunchtime.

"Then what do you want?" he said.

"God only knows," she said quietly. "God knows. God only knows."

By that time she was really crying and he was sensible enough to let her go on with it for another ten minutes or so. During that time he sat on the ground beside her, mostly staring uneasily across the bracken in fear that somebody he knew would come past and see him there.

That would be a miserable situation to be caught in but as it happened, nobody came. There was in fact hardly a sound on the hilltop and hardly a movement except an occasional late butterfly hovering about the blackberries or a rook or two passing above the pines.

When she had finished crying she sat up. The first thing she did was to begin to wipe off the lipstick. She wiped it off quite savagely, positively scrubbing at it with a handkerchief, until her lips again had that dry brownish undressed look about them.

Then she started to plait her hair. When she had finished one plait she held the end of it in her mouth while she tied it with the cord. Then she did the same with the other. Finally she tossed the two plaits back over her shoulders and, with a rough hand sweep, straightened the rest of her hair flat with her hands.

"There," she said bitterly, "how will that do?"

The bitterness in her voice profoundly shocked him. "It can't be as bad as all that," he said, "can it?"

Her eyes stared at him, blank and sour.

"As bad as all what?"

"Well, whatever — can't you tell me?"

"I've never told anybody," she said. "I wouldn't know how to begin."

He started to say something about how much better it was if you could get these things off your chest when he saw her standing up. Once again, for the second time that morning, he was aware of the splendid yellow shoulders, her tallness and the contradiction of the ridiculous scarlet-fastened pigtails with the rest of her body.

"I'd better get back," she said, "before she starts creating hell at me."

"She?"

"Mother," she said. "Oh, and by the way, I almost forgot. She sent a message for you."

"For me?"

"She says will you be sure to come along on Tuesday evening for a drink? She's having a few friends in. About seven o'clock."

He began to say something about his train not always getting in on time, but she cut him short:

"I think you'd better try and make it if you can. She said to tell you she positively won't take no for an answer."

"Well, I shall have to see —"

"You won't," she said. "You know Mother, don't you?"

"I did know her. Years ago —"

"If you knew her then," she said, "you know her now."

He started to feel uneasy again at that remark and said something about he would do his best and did it include his wife, the invitation?

"Nothing was said about Mrs. Barnfield."

A few minutes later, at the crest of the hill, he was holding her foot in the stirrup while she mounted the pony. There was really no need for that piece of help of his, since she could almost have mounted the animal directly from the ground, but she seemed touched by it and turned and gave him, without a word, a short thankful smile.

This touched him too more than words could possibly have done and he mounted his horse in silence. After that they rode, also in silence, for two hundred yards along the hilltop to where the path forked and she said:

"This is my way back. Thank you for everything. Don't forget Tuesday. I'll get it in the neck if you do."

This again was beyond him and he said simply, raising his cap:

"I'll do what I can. Good-by."

Then, turning to ride away, she gave him an odd miserable little smile and once again he found himself appalled by the ridiculous sight of her sitting on the pony. Somehow the picture was not only fatuous. It struck him as being infinitely lonely too.

"And no more crying now," he said. "No more of that."

She turned, rested one hand on the rump of the pony and stared, not at him but completely and far past him, with empty eyes.

"If you listen carefully," she said, "you'll probably hear me howling across the hill in the nighttime."

5

IT WAS past half past seven and already dark, the following Tuesday evening, when he drove up to the old keeper's cottage on the opposite side of the hill. There were lights in the narrow mullioned windows of the little house but, much to his surprise, no other cars.

Edna Whittington herself came to the door to answer his ring, holding in her left hand a half-empty glass and a cigarette in a bright yellow amber holder.

"Sweet of you, Henry. Absolutely and typically sweet."

As she leaned forward so that he could kiss her first on one cheek and then the other he caught an overpowering fragrance, sickly in the night air. He did not fail to notice too how she called him Henry.

"But come in, Henry, come in, come in, you sweet man. Let's look at you."

He went in and, inside, discovered that the house was empty.

"I'm sorry I'm so late," he said.

With magenta-nailed fingers she took his black Homburg hat and umbrella and laid them on a window sill. "The train lost time." He looked round the room to make perfectly sure, for a second time, about its emptiness. "Has everybody gone?"

"Everybody gone?"

"I thought it was a party."

"Party?" she said. "Whoever said it was a party?"

"Valerie."

"Oh! My little girl," she said. "That little girl of mine. My silly little girl."

He started to say that he thought the girl had been pretty emphatic about the party but Edna Whittington laughed, cutting him short, and said:

"She never gets it right, Henry. Never gets anything right, the silly child, just never gets it right."

"Isn't she here either?"

"Out to a little birthday party," she said. "Just a teeny-weeny affair."

She poured him a glass of sherry. Her voice was husky. It was nearly twenty-five years since he had seen her before and he remembered, in time, that the voice had always been husky.

"Well, cheers, Henry," she said. "Resounding numbers of cheers. Lots of luck."

She raised her glass, looking at him with chilled, squinting, remarkably white-blue eyes. Her hair was bluish too and there were shadows of blue, almost violet, in the powder on her face. Her chest, flattish, was steely and bare, except for a double row of pearls, to the beginnings of the creased pouches of her breasts, and her face had a strange bony prettiness except in the mouth, which twisted upward at one side.

"Come and sit here on the sofa and tell me all about yourself. Tell me about life. Here, dear man — not there. Just the old Henry — afraid something will bite you."

He did not think, he said, as he sat beside her on the settee, that he had anything very much of himself to tell; or of life, for that matter.

"Well, I have," she said. "Here we've been in the neighborhood six months and not a bleat from you."

"I honestly didn't know you were here."

"Then you honestly should have done. It was in all the papers. I mean about the colonel. Didn't you read about that?"

He had to confess, with growing wretchedness, that he hadn't even read in the papers about the colonel, who had dropped down of thrombosis a year before. Nevertheless he was, he said, very sorry. It was a sad thing, that.

"He'd got awfully fat," she said. "And of course marrying late and so on. He was a man of forty-five before Valerie was born."

He knew that it was not only the colonel but she too who had married very late. He sat thinking of this, sipping his sherry, watching a meager fire of birch logs smouldering in the round black grate, and she said:

"Yes, I call it pretty stodgy, Henry. Two miles away and not a single lamb's peep out of you. The trouble is you live in a stewpot."

"Now here, I say —"

"Well, don't you? Up to town with *The Times* in the morning. Down from town with *The Standard* in the evening. If that isn't stewpotism tell me what is. Doesn't anything else go on in these parts?"

"Oh, blow it!" he said. "It isn't as bad as that."

"Isn't it?" she said. "I think it's absolutely fungoid."

He suddenly felt very slightly incensed at this and went on to explain, as calmly as he could, how you sometimes held parties, had people to dinner, went in spring to the point-to-points and, damn it, in winter, hunted quite a lot. He didn't think you could call that stewpotism, could you?

"There's the Hunt Ball in a month's time too," he reminded her finally. "You can chalk that up for a whale of a time."

"I would," she said, "if anybody had invited me."

Before he realized what he was saying, he said:

"I'll invite you. Both of you. Delighted."

"Oh, the child could never come."

"No?"

He could not think why on earth the girl could never come.

"She's a mere infant, Henry. Hardly out of the shell. She never does these things. Besides, I'd never let her."

"Why?"

"Oh, Henry, she isn't fledged! She's only half grown. She isn't fit for that sort of thing. You know what these Hunt affairs are too. Wolf packs. Those gangs are not Hunts for nothing."

In his direct, harmless, simple way, the way in which, as everybody always said, there was never any malice, he said:

"But you'd come, wouldn't you?"

"Like a lamplighter, Henry. Absolutely adore to."

He began to murmur something in polite satisfaction about this when she added:

"That's if Katey wouldn't explode."

"I don't think Katey would mind."

That, he always thought, was one nice thing about Katey. She was a good sport, Katey: never jealous in that way.

"And how," she said, "is Katey?"

He shrugged his shoulders: as if there were nothing of very great moment to tell of Katey.

"Tell me about her, Henry," she said. "You can tell me."

There was nothing, he thought, that he possibly wanted to tell.

"I'm sorry," she said, "have I boobed? I simply thought — well, people talk and you know how it is. Somehow I got the impresh — well, you know the impresh one gets — that you and Katey weren't pulling all that steamingly well in harness."

He was roused by the increasing absurdity of her language. She was like a piece of wedding cake that one finds in a silvered box, in a forgotten drawer, among silver leaves, thirty years after the voices at the wedding have faded away. The brittle archaisms of the language were like the hard tarnished silver balls left on the cake. They had seemed so magnificently bright in his youth but now — Good God, had he and Edna and the rest of them really talked like that? If it hadn't been for that absurd, husky clipping voice of hers he would never have believed they had.

As if her thoughts were running in the same direction she said:

"We had some great times, Henry. You and I and Vicky Burton and Freddie Anstruther and Peggy Forbes and Carol Chalmers and Floaty Dean — he was a bright moonbeam, Floaty — do you ever hear anything of any of the crowd?"

"I'm afraid I've lost touch with all of them."

"Well, not all, Henry. Don't say that. You haven't lost touch with me."

Here, as so often in the conversation, she smiled, played with the pearls above the thin steely bosom or extended, to its full length, the arm holding the dying cigarette in its yellow holder.

"Do you remember a day on the river at Pangbourne?"

He pretended not to remember it while, in reality, remembering it very well. That day she had worn her pale yellow hair in a bob and a hat like a round pink saucepan. Her white dress had been short and waistless, revealing round and pretty knees below the skirt.

There was no doubt in his mind that she too had been very pretty; and she said:

"But you remember coming home, through the woods? You wanted to go with Carol but I wanted you to come with me. All the rhododendrons were out, big white and pale pink ones so that you could see them in the dark, and I made an honest man of you."

She laughed distastefully.

"You *surely* don't forget, Henry, do you?" she said. "After all, it was the first time with you and me, even if it wasn't the last, and you know how — "

"Look, Edna, we were all a bit crazy at that time and I don't think we have to drag it all — "

He was relieved to hear the sound of car brakes in the

road outside. Then he heard a car door slam and the sound of feet running up the path outside.

A moment later Valerie Whittington came in. She was wearing a blue gabardine school mackintosh and a plain gray felt hat and white ankle socks above her plain flat shoes. The mackintosh was too long for her by several inches and when she started to take it off he saw that underneath it she was wearing a plain dark blue dress that was full and bushy in the skirt. It too was too long for her.

"Well, there you are at last, child. Say good evening to Mr. Barnfield before you go up. I know you know him because he was kind enough to let you use the path."

"Good evening, Mr. Barnfield."

He said good evening too and knew, as he did so, that she had the greatest difficulty in looking at him. He tried in vain to catch the big, brown, too-circular eyes.

"Well, up you go now, child. It's late. It's past your time. Say good night to Mr. Barnfield."

"Good night, Mr. Barnfield."

He nodded. He thought she made a sort of timid, half-urgent effort to protest but she turned away too quickly, leaving him unsure. The last visible sign of what she might be thinking was a shudder of her lower lip, hard and quite convulsive, just before she turned, opened the door and went out without a word.

"I must go too," he said.

"Oh, not yet, Henry. Have another sherry — "

"No, no," he said. "Really, no, no. Katey will have dinner —"

"Give her a ping on the blower and say you'll be another half hour. We've hardly exchanged the sliver of a word —"

"No, honestly, Edna," he said. "Honestly I must go."

She came with him, at last, to the door. In the light from the door she stood for a moment gauntly, thinly framed, a piece of silver cardboard, and he thought again of the wedding cake. Then she half closed the door behind her. The October air was mild and windless but as she stretched out long fleshless arms to say good-by he said hastily:

"Don't come out. Don't get cold. I'm perfectly capable —"

"Good night, Henry," she said. "Sweet of you to come. And that's a date, then, isn't it — the ball?"

"That's if you'd care —"

"Oh, Henry!" She laughed huskily. "Care?"

She offered her face to be kissed. He made as if to inflict on it, somewhere between cheek and ear, a swift dab of farewell. The next moment he felt her thin fingers grasp him about the elbows. Then they moved up to his shoulders and suddenly she was offering her mouth instead.

"You can do better than that, Henry, can't you?" she

said. She laughed with what he supposed she thought was tenderness. Her voice crackled on its rising note with a brittle snap. "I know you can. From what I remember of the rhododendrons. And not only the rhododendrons."

"Look, Edna, I've already told you. That's all over long since," he said, and escaped, leaving her mouth in air.

6

HE WAS SURPRISED, the following Sunday morning, to see no sign of the yellow sweater among the brushwood jumps in the meadows.

"Your girl friend has passed you up," Katey said. "She hasn't been near all week, so Lewis says."

After breakfast he rode out to the meadow and jumped for half an hour in cool exhilarating air, across grass still white-wet from frost. In the hedgerows leaves of maple and hornbeam were growing every day more and more like clear light candle flame and up on the hill the beeches were burning deeper and deeper, fox-fiery beyond the pines, against ice-blue autumn sky.

The hill was irresistible and finally he rode up, slowly, in bright sunshine, about eleven o'clock, through acres of dying bracken and birches that were shedding, in pure silence, after the night frost, the gentlest yellow fall of leaves.

One or two people were walking on the crest of the

hill but no one except himself was riding and he was half
in mind to turn the horse, ride down the opposite hillside
as far as the Black Boy and treat himself to a whisky there
at twelve o'clock, when he suddenly saw walking across
the bracken a tall figure in a black skirt and a puce-pink
blouse.

It was a pigtailless, hatless, horseless Valerie Whittington, waving her hand.

"I thought it must be you," she said and even he was
not too stupid to know that she must have been waiting
for him there.

"Where's your pony?" he said.

"I've stopped riding."

"Oh?"

It was all he could think of to say as he raised his cap,
dismounted and stood beside her.

He saw at once that she was wearing lipstick. She had
also managed to bunch up her hair into thick brown
curls and to make an effort to match the color of her face
to the puce pink of the blouse. Except for the evening at
the cottage he had not seen her in skirts before and now
he saw that her legs were long, well shaped and slender.

"Given up riding?" he said. "How is that?"

"I've just given up riding," she said.

Even from the tone of this remark he saw that she had
changed a great deal. Like her voice, her face was grave,
almost solemn. Her eyes seemed queer and distant.

"Have you time to walk a little way?" she said.

He said yes, he had time, and they walked slowly, in cool sunshine, he leading the horse, to where he could see once again the entire valley of oak woods and pasture below. In a few weeks he would be hunting across it, drinking the first sharp draughts of winter.

"I'm afraid I behaved like a fool up here the other day," she said, "and I'm sorry about the other night."

He said he couldn't think why.

"Well, it's all over now," she said, "but I just wanted to say."

Exactly what, he asked, was all over now?

"Me," she said. "I'm leaving home. I'm going away."

It was instantly typical of him to ask her if she thought that was wise.

"Wise or not," she said, "I'm going."

Everybody wanted to run away when they were young, he said, but it was like measles. You got over it in time and you were probably all the better for having been through the wretched thing.

"Yes, I'm better," she said. "Because I know where I'm going now. Thanks to you."

He couldn't think what he possibly had to do with it and she said:

"I like being with you. I grow up when I'm with you. Somehow you never take me away from myself."

This odd, solemn little pronouncement of hers affected

him far more than her tears had ever done and he glanced quickly at her face. It was full of another, different kind of tearfulness, dry and barren, with a pinched sadness that started dragging at his heart.

"You know what I've been doing since last Sunday?" she said.

"No."

"Coming up here."

"Yes?"

"Every day," she said. "Walking. Not with the pony — I haven't ridden the pony since that day. Just walking. I think I know every path here now. There's a wonderful one goes down past the holly trees. You come to a little lake at the bottom with quince trees on an island — at least I think they're quince trees."

If he had time, she went on, she wanted him to walk down there. Would he? Did he mind?

He tethered his horse to a fence and they started to walk along a path that wound down, steeply in places, through crackling curtains of bracken, old holly trees thick with pink-brown knots of berry and more clumps of birch trees sowing in absolute silence little yellow pennies of leaves.

At the bottom there was, as she had said, a small perfectly circular lake enclosed by rings of alder, willow and hazel trees. In the still air its surface was thick with floating shoals of leaves. In absolute silence two quince trees, half-bare branches full of ungathered golden lamps of fruit, shone with apparent permanent candescence on a little island in the glow of noon.

"This is it," she said.

Neither then, nor later, nor in fact at any other time, did they say a word about her mother. They stood for a long time without a word about anything, simply watching the little lake soundlessly embalmed in October sunlight, the quince lamps setting the little island half on fire.

"I don't think you should go away," he said.

"Why not?"

He answered her in the quiet, totally uncomplex way that, as everyone so often remarked, was so much a part of him, so much the typical Harry Barnfield.

"I don't want you to," he said.

She started to say something and then stopped. He looked at her face. He thought suddenly that it had lost the dry, barren tearfulness. Now it looked uncomplicated, alight and free. The big glowing brown eyes seemed to embrace him with a wonderful look of gratitude.

"What were you going to say?" he said.

"Nothing."

"You were."

"I was," she said, "but now it doesn't matter."

All at once she laid her hands on his shoulders, drawing them slowly down until, quite nervously, she plucked

at the lapels of his jacket. In shyness she could not look
at him. She could only stare at her own fingers as she
drew them slowly up and down.

Suddenly she let them fly up to his uncertain, spectacled, honest face with a breaking cry.

"Oh, my God, hold me!" she said. "Hold me — just
hold me, will you? — for God's sake please just hold
me —"

In a stupid daze Harry Barnfield held her; and from
across the lake the sound of a duck's wing flapping somewhere about the island of quinces reached him, long
afterwards, like the echo of a stone dropping far away at
the bottom of a well.

7

Soon, as the autumn went on, his friends the city gentlemen began to notice a strange, unforetold change in his
habits. No longer was it possible, several days a week,
to wait with expectation and cheers to put the grappling
hooks on Harry Barnfield as he ran, spectacled and panting, to catch the evening train.

The reason for this was a simple one: Harry Barnfield
was, on these evenings, not there to be grappled.

By the time the train departed he was already away in
the country, saying good-by to the girl on the hillside or,
in bad weather, as they sat in his car by the road. A train

at two-thirty gave him an hour or more before, at six o'clock, he watched her, with a dry twist in his heart, walk away into twilights filled more and more with storms of blowing leaves.

Earlier in the afternoon they walked by the little lake. As late as the first week in November the lamps of the quinces hung miraculously suspended from the gray central islands of boughs and then gradually, one by one, dropped into the frosted reeds below.

By the middle of November there remained, on the south side of the island, where the sun caught it full in the early afternoons, one quince, the last of the autumn lanterns, and as Harry Barnfield and the girl came down the path through thinning alder trees she got into the way of running on ahead of him to the edge of the lake, always giving the same little cry:

"Look, Harry, our quince is still there!"

For about a week longer they watched, as if it were some marvelously suspended planet glowing above the wintry stretches of water where thin ice sometimes lingered white all day in the thickest shadow of reeds, the last remaining quince, suspended bare and yellow on frost-stripped boughs.

"When it falls I shall feel the summer has gone completely," the girl said.

Soon Harry Barnfield felt as she did: that this was the last of summer poured into a single phial of honey. When it fell and split at last he knew he would hear, dark and snapping, the breath of winter.

By the fifteenth day of the month the quince, looking bigger and more golden than ever in an afternoon of pure, almost shrill blue sky already touched on the horizon by the coppery threat of frost, still remained.

"Look, Harry!" the girl said. "Our quince is still there!"

For some time they walked slowly by the lake. In the breathless blue afternoon the one remaining globe of fruit glowed more than ever like the distillation of all the summer.

"It's nearly two months now," the girl said, "since we first came down here. Have you been happy?"

He started to say that he had never been so happy in his life but she cut him short and said:

"What made you happy?"

He could not think what had made him happy except, perhaps, that he had been freed, at last, from the shackles of his daily ride in the train, the banterings of the city gentlemen and above all from the evening crackle of Katey's voice calling that she hoped to God he hadn't forgotten the gin. But before he had time to reply the girl said:

"I'll tell you why it is. It's because you've made someone else happy. Me, in fact."

"I'm glad about that."

"You see," she said, "it's like shining a light. You shine it and it reflects back at you."

"But supposing," he said in his simple, straightforward way, "there's nothing to reflect back from?"

"Oh, but there is!" she said. "There's me."

He smiled at this and a moment later she stopped, touched his arm and said:

"I wonder if you feel about it the same way as I do? I feel in a wonderful way that you and I have been growing up together."

He hadn't a second in which to answer this odd remark before, across the lake, the quince fell with a thud, almost a punch, into the reeds below. The sound startled the girl so much that she gave a sudden dismaying gasp:

"Oh! Harry, it's gone! Our quince has gone — oh! Harry, look, it's empty without it!"

He stared across to the island and saw that it was, as she said, quite empty.

"Now," she said, "it's winter."

He thought he caught for the briefest possible moment a colder breath of air rising from the lake, but it was in fact her shadow crossing his face, shutting out the sun, as she turned and looked at him.

"The quince has gone and it's winter," she said. "The week has gone and tomorrow it's Friday. Have you forgotten?"

"Friday?" he said. "Forgotten?"

"Friday," she said, "is the Hunt Ball."

"Good God, I'd forgotten," he said.

Now it was her turn to smile and she said:

"Whatever you do you mustn't forget. You simply mustn't. You're coming to fetch us. Will you dance with me?"

"If —" He was about to say "If your mother will let you," but he checked himself in time and said, "If you don't mind being trodden on. It's some time since I danced, especially to modern things."

"I've a new dress," she said.

There crossed his mind the picture of her coming home, as he vividly remembered it, from the birthday party: the dress long, straight and blue under the blue school mackintosh; and he felt his heart once again start to ache for her, afraid of what she would wear.

"Nobody has seen it," she said.

It was on the tip of his tongue to say "Not even —" when he checked himself again and she said:

"I hope you'll like me in it. Nobody knows about it. I bought it alone, by myself. It's the color of — No, I won't tell you after all. You'll see it tomorrow and then you can tell me if it reminds you of something."

Suddenly she stretched up her arms in a short delightful gesture.

"You will dance with me," she said, "won't you? A lot?"

"I warn you — " he said, and then: "I'm pretty awful."

"I don't believe it," she said. "Show me. Dance with me now."

For the second time she held up her arms. She put her left arm lightly on his shoulder and he took her other hand.

"I'll hum the tune," she said. "Listen carefully."

She started humming something but although he listened carefully he could not recognize at all what tune it was.

"You'll have to guide me," she said. "My eyes are shut. I always dance with my eyes shut. And by the way, next week I'm twenty. Ancient. Had you forgotten?"

He had forgotten about that too.

"You dance nicely — very nicely — we go together — nicely — very nicely together —"

She started to sing the words to the tune she was humming, the tune he did not recognize, and as he danced to it, steering her about the frost-bared path along the lake, he remembered the sound of the quince dropping into the reeds, the last vanishing phial of the summer's honey, filling his mind like a golden ominous echo.

8

WHEN HE CALLED alone at the keeper's cottage next evening about half past eight he saw at once that all his fears were justified. It was she who opened the door; and already, as he saw, she was wearing the blue school mackintosh. He even thought he caught, as she turned her head, a glimpse of two pigtails tucked inside the half-turned-up collar at the back.

Nervously picking first at his silk evening scarf and then his black Homburg hat he stood in the little sitting room and wished, for once, that Edna was there.

"Mother will be a few minutes yet," the girl said. "She always takes an awful time. She said I was to give you sherry. Or is there something else you'd rather have?"

He was about to say that sherry would suit him perfectly when she smiled, leaned close to him and said:

"This, for instance?"

She kissed him lightly. Her lips, not made up, with that curious undressed brownish look about them, rested on his mouth for no more than a second or two and then drew away.

"How many dances," she said, "are you going to dance with me?"

"Well —"

"Dance with me all evening."

"I shall have to dance with your mother —"

"Dance once with Mother and then all the rest with me." Again she kissed him lightly on the lips. "All night. Forever. Dance with me forever."

Miserably, a few moments later, he took the glass of sherry she poured out for him.

"I'm not allowed to drink," she said. "But I'm going to. Mother will be ages."

With increasing wretchedness he saw her pour another glass of sherry, hold it up to him and say:

"Do you know what I used to say when I was a child and wanted to describe something that was very, very good?"

"No."

"I used to call it the bestest good one." She laughed with large shining eyes and drank half the sherry in a gulp. "Here's to our evening. May it be the bestest good one in the world."

All this time she kept the blue gabardine school mackintosh closely buttoned at the neck. He would not have been surprised to see that her stockings were black, though in fact they were flesh-colored, and once he found himself looking down at her black flat-heeled shoes.

"Oh! That reminds me," she said. "Would you hide these in the car for me? They're my dancing shoes."

He took the brown paper parcel she gave him and went out to the car and put the parcel on the back seat.

The night was starry and crisp, with a half moon in the west.

Immediately, as he got back to the house, he heard the husky voice of Edna Whittington asking where he was.

In the sitting room she greeted him with outstretched thin bare arms, fingers crooked.

"Henry. I thought you were leaving us, trotting out there in the cold. I thought my little girl wasn't looking after you."

She was wearing a skin-tight dress that looked, he thought, as if it were made of silver mail. It made her look more than ever like a sere cardboard leaf left over from a wedding cake. Her long fingernails and her lips were a sharp magenta and the skin of her chest and face was powdered to a rosy-violet shade.

"No Katey?"

Her voice was full of petulant mock regret.

He apologized and said that Katey was, on the whole, not a great one for dancing.

"Poor Katey. Well, anyway, all the more luck for me."

In the intervals of talking and, he thought, smiling too much, she poured herself a glass of sherry and then filled up his own. All this time the girl stood apart, school-girlish, meek, hands in pockets of her mackintosh, not speaking.

"Henry," Edna Whittington said, "it's terribly sweet of

you to take us to this thing and it's mean of me to ask another favor. But would you?"

"Of course."

"What time does this affair break up?"

"Oh, hard to say," he said. "Three or four. I've known it to be five."

"Shambles?"

"Quite often," he said. "Well, it's the Hunt Ball and you know how people are."

"I know how people are and that's why I wanted to ask you. Would you," she said, "be an absolute lamb and bring Valerie back by one o'clock? I've promised her she can come on that one condition."

"If you think —"

"I do think and you're an absolute lamb. She doesn't mind being alone in the house and then you can come back for me and we'll stay on to the end."

The girl did not speak or move. Her large brown eyes were simply fixed straight ahead of her, as if she actually hadn't heard.

Ten minutes later the three of them drove off, Edna Whittington sitting beside him at the wheel, wearing only a white long silk shawl as a wrap, the girl at the back, motionless and obliterated in the darkness, without a word.

"Oh! Look! They've floodlit the mansion! The whole place looks like a wedding cake!"

As he turned the car into tall high park gates Edna Whittington's voice ripped at the night air with a husky tear. At the end of a long avenue of bare regiments of chestnut a great house seemed to stare with a single candescent eye, pure white, across black spaces of winter parkland. And as the car drew nearer he thought that it looked, as she said, like a wedding cake, just as she herself, thin, shining and silver, looked more than ever like a leaf of it that had been long since torn away.

Less than ten minutes later he was inside the long central hall of the mansion, bright with chandeliers and crowded already with dancers, many of them his acquaintances of the hunting field, some his friends the city gentlemen, hearing Edna Whittington say with a smile of her bony once pretty magenta mouth:

"It's over twenty years since I danced with you, Henry, and I can't wait to have a quick one. What are they playing? What are you looking at?"

"I was wondering," he said, "where Valerie had —"

A moment later, before he could complete the sentence or she could answer it, he felt himself pressed to the thin sheer front of her body and borne away.

9

It might have been half an hour, perhaps only twenty minutes, when he turned in the middle of the second of

his dances with Edna Whittington and became the victim
of exactly the same kind of momentary illusion that he
had suffered one brilliant Sunday morning in the cucumber house.

For a second or two, out of the corner of his eye, he
thought he saw a strange but remotely recognizable fragment of yellow light cross a far corner of the room and
disappear behind a triangular tier of pink chrysanthemums.

He was suddenly stunned to realize that this was Valerie Whittington, wearing a remarkably long pale yellow
dress and long black gloves that showed her pale bare upper
arms and her completely naked back and shoulders. He
was so numbed by this appearance that only one thought
raced through his head, in reality the rapid recollection of
something she had said by the lake on the previous
afternoon:

"Nobody knows about it. It's the color of — No, I
won't tell you. You'll see it tomorrow and then you can
tell me if it reminds you of anything."

Instantly he recalled the quinces and how the lamp of
summer had gone out.

Somehow he got through the rest of the dance without
betraying that he was in a turmoil of fright and indecision.

He had broken out already into a cold and sickening
sweat but as the dance ended he had presence of mind

enough to mop his forehead with his handkerchief and say:

"It's awfully hot in here, Edna. My glasses are getting misty. Do you mind if I go and clean them? And wouldn't you like a drink? Can I bring you something — gin and something? — would you? — by all means, yes —"

He escaped, spent five minutes in an empty back corridor breathing on his spectacles, polishing them and then in sheer fright breathing on them again. After that he worked his way to the corner of the bar and restored himself with a whisky, saying desperately at the last moment:

"No, a large one, large one please."

Then he took the drink back into the corridor. He had hardly leaned against the wall and had actually not lifted the glass to his lips when he looked up and saw Valerie Whittington suddenly appear at the far end of the corridor as if she had in some miraculous way come up through a trap door.

She started to walk towards him. She walked quite slowly, upright, shoulders square and splendid, the motion of her legs just breaking the front of the dress with ripples. And across the vision of her walking slowly down towards him he caught for the flash of a second the former vision of her in the gabardine mackintosh, schoolgirlish, tense and obliterated, the pigtails tucked into the collar at the back.

A moment later she was saying:

"I know what you're thinking. You're thinking did I have it on under the mackintosh, aren't you?"

"Partly that —"

"I hadn't," she said. "It was easy. I got the shop to send it here. I'd hardly a thing on under the mackintosh."

She started to smile. Her lips were made up, a pale red, and she had managed once again to pile her hair into a mass of curls. She did not speak again for a moment or two. She continued to smile at him with the large circular brown eyes that so often seemed to embrace him with tenderness and then at last she said:

"Does it remind you of anything?"

"Of course," he said.

To his surprise the two words seemed to move her very deeply and he saw that there were sudden tears in her eyes.

"You're the bestest good one in the world," she said and she pressed her face against his own.

He too found himself very moved by that. He wished he had nothing to do but take her by one of the long black gloves and into the dark spaces of parkland outside the house, but he remembered Edna Whittington.

Some of his anxiety about this must have crossed his face because almost immediately she said:

"I'll tell you something else you're thinking too, shall I?"

Harry Barnfield, only too well aware of what he was thinking, could not answer.

"You're thinking you've got to dance with me."

"Well — "

He inclined his head a fraction down and away from her. When he looked up at her again he was struck by a wonderful air of composure about her face, the wide bare shoulders and especially the hands, black in their gloves, clasped lightly before the waistline of the yellow dress. She could not have looked more composed if she had been wearing the dress for the fiftieth instead of the first time but he knew, somehow, in spite of it all, that she was frightened.

"It's got to be done," she said, "and I can't do it without you."

He tried not to look into her eyes. They were no longer wet with even the suspicion of tears. They gazed back at him, instead, with an almost luminous composure and now, at last, she stretched out her hands.

"Come along," she said. "Take me."

If there had been no other person on the dance floor as he led her on to it some moments later he could hardly have felt more pained and conspicuous. It was like dancing in some sort of competition, naked, in the middle of an empty field, before a thousand spectators.

The amazing thing was that whenever he looked at the

face of the girl it was still alight with that astonishing luminous composure.

"Look at me," she said once. "Keep looking at me."

Whether she was thinking of her mother, as he was the whole time, he did not know. He could not see Edna Whittington. But as he danced he became more and more obsessed with the haunting impression that she was watching him from somewhere, evilly and microscopically, waiting for the dance to end.

When it did end he turned helplessly on the floor, arms still outstretched, very much like a child learning to walk and suddenly deprived of a pair of helping hands. The girl, composed as ever, started to move away, the skin of her back shining golden in the light of the chandeliers. The dress itself looked, as she had meant it to do, more than ever the color of quinces and he saw on her bare arms a bloom of soft down like that on the skin of the fruit.

Then as she turned, smiled at him with an amazing triumphant serenity, holding out her arm for him to take, he saw Edna Whittington.

She was standing not far from the tier of pink chrysanthemums. She did not look, now, like a piece of silver cardboard. She looked exactly like the perfectly straight double-edged blade of a dagger rammed point downwards into the floor: arms perfectly crossed, feet close together, thin body perfectly motionless under the tight silver dress, small microscopic eyes staring straight forward out of a carved white face, fixed on himself and the girl as they crossed the dance floor.

Suddenly he was no longer uneasy, self-conscious or even disturbed. He began to feel strangely confident, almost antagonistic. And in this sudden change of mood he felt himself guide the arm of the girl, changing her course across the dance floor, steering her straight to Edna Whittington.

Suddenly the band started playing again. The girl gave a quick little cry of delight, turned to him and put her hands on his shoulders. A moment later they were dancing.

Then, for what was to be the last time, she spoke of her mother.

"Is she looking?"

"Yes."

"Tell me how she looks," she said. "You know I dance with my eyes closed."

"There's no need to think of her."

Whether it was because of this simple remark of his he never knew, but suddenly she rested her face against his and spoke to him in a whisper.

"You don't know how happy I am," she said. "Oh! Don't wake me, will you? Please don't wake me."

She spoke once more as they danced and it was also in a whisper.

"If I told you I loved you here in the middle of this dance floor would you think it ridiculous?"

"That's the last thing I would ever think."

"I love you," she said.

At the end of the dance a frigid, pale supernaturally polite Edna Whittington, holding a glittering yellow cigarette holder in full-stretched magenta fingers, met them as they came from the floor. Rigidly and antagonistically he held himself ready to do some sort of brave and impossible battle with her and was surprised to hear her say:

"You did book our table for supper, didn't you, Henry?"

"Of course."

"You should have told me where it was," she said. "Then I could have sat down."

Throughout the rest of the evening, until one o'clock, this was as sharp as the tone of her reproach and resentment ever grew. She regarded himself, the girl, the dancing, and even the dress, with the same unmitigated calm. When he danced with her, as he did several times, she talked with a kind of repressed propriety, saying such things as:

"It's a most pleasant evening, Henry. And not noisy. Not a brawl. Not half as crowded as I thought it would be."

"The Hunt's going through a difficult patch," he said. "Rather going down, I'm afraid. There isn't the interest. There aren't the chaps."

"You seem to know a lot of people, even so."

The more polite and calm she grew the more unreal, he thought, the night became. Alternately he danced with herself and the girl. Friendly and bantering from across the floor came exchanges of manly pleasantry with friends like Punch Warburton, Freddie Jekyll and George Reed Thompson, the city gentlemen, from odd acquaintances like Dr. Frobisher, Justice Smythe and Colonel Charnly-Rose: stalwart chaps, the solid backbone of the Hunt.

Away somewhere in the distance lay the even greater unreality of Katey: Katey drowned throughout the years of his marriage in mists of gin, Katey the tawdry lioness, Katey with her garlic-raw, smoke-stained fingers, calling him a squeak-mouse.

He felt himself left, over and over again, with the one reality of his life that had ever meant anything. All the rest had shriveled behind him like black burned paper. Nothing made any sense in any sort of way any more, except the voice of the girl imploring him with the tenderest, most luminous happiness:

"Oh! Don't wake me, will you? Please don't wake me."

It would be the best possible thing now, he thought, to get it over quickly: to go straight to Katey, in the morning, and tell her what had happened and how, because of it, he could not go on with the old, damnable dreary business any longer.

He had arrived at this, the simplest of decisions, by midnight, when Edna Whittington, the girl and himself sat down to supper. To his relief and surprise it was a remarkably pleasant supper. He poured champagne and the girl, unreproached, was allowed to drink it. He fetched, with his own hands, as she and her mother expressed their fancy, plates of cold chicken or salmon, frozen strawberries and ice cream, mousse and mayonnaise.

"Did I see someone with pineapple *gâteau*, Henry?" Edna Whittington said and he went dutifully to search for it, pursued by a voice of unbelievably husky-sweet encouragement: "And be a lamb and find cream, Henry, if you can. Dancing makes me hungry."

In the next hour the wine, the food and the utter absence of malignity in all that Edna Whittington said or did had lured him into a state where he was no longer apprehensive or uncertain or even ready to go into brave and antagonistic battle against her.

In consequence he was as unprepared as a rabbit sitting before a stoat when, at one o'clock, Edna Whittington looked at her watch, then at the girl, then at himself and said:

"Child, it's time for you to go home. Henry, are you ready to take her?"

10

THE GIRL did not move. He felt the ease of the evening shatter with an ugly crack. His nerves upheld his skin with minute pin pricks of actual pain.

"I said it was time to go home, child. Get your things. Put your coat on. Mr. Barnfield will take you."

The girl still did not move or speak. Looking at her, he was reminded of the first morning he had ever met her. The innocent insolence had come back to her face again and he understood it now.

"Valerie."

Edna Whittington waited. He lifted his glass, drank some champagne and waited too The girl still did not move. She sat with black gloves composed and crossed on the table in front of her. Her eyes, not so wide and circular as they often were, looked half down at her hands, half at the dance floor. Just above the cut of the yellow dress her breasts started to rise and fall rather quickly but otherwise she did not stir.

"I am not in the habit of telling you twice," Edna Whittington said. The voice was icy. "Get your things at once and go home."

The band had begun playing. He clenched the stem of his glass, then relaxed his fingers and looked straight at the ice-gray microscopic eyes of Edna Whittington.

"She's not going home," he said.

"Will you please mind your own business?"

He found himself drawing on remarkable reserves of calm, backed by the echo of a voice which kept saying "I feel in a wonderful way that we've been growing up together."

"Child!"

"I have told you, Edna, that she is not going home."

"Will you kindly mind your own business!"

He lifted his face, pushed his glass aside and looked straight into the eyes of the girl.

"Shall we dance?" he said.

She hesitated for a fraction of a second. He thought he saw at the same time an indecipherable shadow run across her face, as if she were actually in a turmoil of indecision. And for a moment he was in horror that she would fail, break down and go home.

Instead she smiled and got up. As the skirt of the yellow dress moved into full view from below the table he remembered the shining lamp of the solitary remaining quince burning in the blue November glassiness above the lake on cooling crystal afternoons, the last phial of the summer's honey, and he knew that now, at last, there was no need to doubt her.

A moment later they were dancing. They danced per-

haps twice around the room before she even looked or
spoke to him. Then slowly she lifted her face, staring at
him as if she could not see him distinctly.

"You're the bestest good one," she said. "The most
bestest good one in the world."

And as she spoke he found, suddenly, that he could
not bear to look at her. Her huge brown eyes were
drowned in tears of happiness.

11

IT WAS NEARLY three o'clock when Edna Whittington said
to him in a husky discordant voice that betrayed, at last,
the first snap of anger:

"If you feel you've enjoyed yourself enough I should
like to go home."

"I'm ready whenever you are," he said. "Shall I take
you alone or shall we all go together?"

She paused before answering; and he thought for a
moment that she was going to laugh, as she sometimes
did, distastefully. Instead she picked the minutest shred
of tobacco from her mouth, looked at it and then flicked
it away.

"We'll go together," she said. "I want to talk to you."

"As far as I'm concerned there's nothing to talk about."

"She's my daughter," she said, "and I want to talk to you."

"Very well, Edna," he said. "Talk to me."

"I'll talk to you," she said, "at home."

They drove home in frosty darkness, under a starry sky from which the moon had gone down. The girl sat in the back of the car, as before, and no one spoke a word.

When he pulled up before the cottage no one, for nearly half a minute, moved either.

"Will you come in?" Edna Whittington said at last.

"No thank you."

"Then I'll talk to you here." She turned to the girl. "Go inside, Valerie. Here's the key."

The girl did not move or answer. Harry Barnfield turned, saw her sitting there motionless, mackintoshless, cool in the yellow dress, and said:

"Better go." He took the key of the cottage from Edna Whittington and handed it to the girl. "I think it's better."

"I'm going," she said very quietly. "Good night. See you tomorrow."

Then, and he could only guess what it cost her to do it, the girl leaned over, turned his head with her hand and kissed him on the lips, saying:

"Thank you for everything. Good night."

Before he could move to open the door for her she was out of the car, running. He heard the key scrape in the lock of the cottage door. Then the door opened and shut and he was alone, in silence, with Edna Whittington.

He said at once: "I don't know what you have to say, Edna, but it's very late and I'd like to get home."

"How long has this been going on?" she said.

"About twenty years."

"If you're going to be flippant I shall probably lose my temper and —"

"I'm not going into explanations," he said, "if that's what you want, and the sooner you get it into your head the better."

She gave the distasteful beginning of a laugh.

"All right. I'll just ask you one question. If that isn't too much?"

"Ask."

"I suppose you're going to tell me you love this child?"

"Very much."

"Setting aside the word infatuation," she said, "do you suppose she loves you?"

"I do, and she does," he said.

This time she did laugh. It was husky, unpleasant and briefly sinister.

"I honestly think you're serious about this."

"I'm not only serious," he said. "It's my whole life. And hers."

She started to light a cigarette. He disliked very much the idea of smoking in cars and he was annoyed as he saw

the thin masked face, so drawn that it was almost skele-
tonized, in the light of the match and then in the burning
glow of the cigarette held between the drooping magenta
lips.

"You know, Henry," she said — she blew smoke with
what appeared to be unconstricted ease — "somebody will
have to be told."

He instantly thought of Katey: Katey the shabby lioness, passing through her blond phases, her gin mists;
Katey yelling at him, calling him a squeak-mouse; messy,
lost, groping, scrofulous Katey.

"Oh! Katey will be told," he said. "I'll tell Katey. Tomorrow."

Edna Whittington blew smoke in a thin excruciated
line.

"I wasn't thinking of Katey."

He couldn't think who else could possibly be told and
for a moment he didn't care.

"I daresay my friends have put two and two together," he
said, "if that's what you mean."

"I wasn't thinking of your friends."

"Who then?"

She drew smoke and released it. The smoke had a
strange repugnant scent about it. He saw her eyes nar-
rowed in the narrow face, the mouth drawn down, almost
cadaverous, and he grasped that this was a smile.

"Valerie," she said. "Valerie will have to be told."

"Told?" he said. The car was half full of smoke, tainted with the scent of it. He felt his annoyance with her rising to temper. "Told what, for God's sake?"

"About us," she said. "You and me."

"Us? And what about us?"

He suddenly felt uneasy and on edge, nerves probing, the smoke sickening him.

"I think she has to be told," she said, "that you and I were lovers. Of course it was some time ago. But wouldn't you think that that was only fair?"

He could not speak. He simply made one of his habitual groping gestures with his hands, up towards his face, as if his spectacles had suddenly become completely opaque with the white sickening smoke of her cigarette and he could not see.

"Not once," she said, "but many times. "Oh, yes, I think she has to be told. I think so."

She did not know quite what happened after that. He seemed suddenly to lose control of himself and started yelling. She had never known a Harry Barnfield who could yell, show anger, make foul noises or use violence and now he struck her in the face. The blow partially blinded her, knocking the cigarette from her lips, and in the confusion she heard him yelling blackly as he turned the key of the car.

When she recovered herself the car was traveling down the road, very fast. As it turned under dark trees by a bend, she realized that the headlights were not on. He was bent forward over the wheel, glaring wildly through the thickish spectacles into a half darkness from which trees rushed up like gaunt shadows.

"I'll kill you, I'll kill you," he kept saying. "I'll kill you first."

She started screaming. Out of the darkness sprang a re-membered figure of a Harry Barnfield in a white straw hat, white flannel trousers and a college blazer, a rather soft Harry Barnfield, simple, easygoing, good-time-loving, defenseless and laughing; one of the vacuous poor fish of her youth, in the days when she had kept a tabulation of conquests in a little book, heading it *In Memoriam: to those who fell,* her prettiness enameled and calculated and as smart as the strip-poker or the midnight swimming par-ties she went to, with other, even younger lovers, at long week ends.

Almost the last thing she remembered was struggling with the door of the car. When at first she could not open it she struck out at Harry Barnfield with her hands. At the second blow she hit him full in the spectacles. She heard them crunch as they broke against the bone of his forehead and then the car door was opening, swinging wide, and she was out of it, half jumping, half falling onto the soft frosted grass of the verge.

The car, driven by a blinded Harry Barnfield, swerved on wildly down the hill. She was conscious enough to

hear a double scream of brakes as it skimmed the bends
and then the crash of glass as it struck, far down, a final
telegraph pole.

12

ON THE AFTERNOON of Harry Barnfield's funeral the
wind rose grayly, mild in sudden rainless squalls, across a
landscape bare of leaves. The heads of many of the
mourners were very bald and as they followed the coffin,
in a long slow line, they gave the appearance of so many
shaven monks solemnly crossing the churchyard.

At the house, afterwards, there were tea and coffee,
with whisky and gin for those who preferred something
stronger. The Hunt was well represented. The city gentlemen, J. B. (Punch) Warburton, Freddie Jekyll and George
Reed Thompson, were there. The sheriff of the county was
represented. The Masters of several other Hunts, two
from a neighboring county, together with three local mag-
istrates and two doctors from the local hospital were
there. Colonel and Mrs. Charnly-Rose, Justice Smythe
and his two daughters, both excellent horsewomen, and
several clergymen, farmers, horse dealers and corn mer-
chants were there. It was impossible to say how many people, from all sections of society, from villagers to men of
title, had come to pay tribute to Harry Barnfield, who, as
everyone knew, was a good huntsman, a good sport, a

great horse-lover and a man in whom there was no harm at all.

In addition to the tea, coffee, whisky and gin there were also cucumber sandwiches and many people said how excellent they were. Several people, as they ate them, walked out of the crowded house into the garden, for a breath of fresh air. Others strolled as far as the edges of the meadows, where Harry Barnfield's horses were grazing and his run of brushwood jumps stood dark and deserted beneath a squally sky.

As they walked they wondered, as people do at funerals, about the future: what would happen, who would get what and above all what Katey would do. Across the fields and the hillside the wind blew into separated threads the wintry blades of grass, over the parched fox-like ruffles of dead bracken and, rising, rattled the gray bones of leafless boughs. "We'll miss him on the five o'clock," the city gentlemen said and confessed that they had no idea what would happen, who would get what or above all what Katey would do.

Nor could anyone possibly hear, in the rising winter wind, in the falling winter darkness, any sound of voices weeping across the hillside in the nighttime.

Night Run to the West

1

HE first met her on an early spring evening when he was doing the night run from London to the West, a journey that he could do in six and a half hours, if things went well, with a full load on the truck. That night he was about halfway, somewhere on the long chalk switchbacks about Salisbury, when he blew a gasket. An almost full moon was shining starkly on the slopes of white hillsides, where leafing bushes of hawthorn looked very much like shadowy herds of cattle crouched and sleeping. It was almost eleven o'clock by that time and he pulled up at the first house he saw.

He was glad to see a light in one window and still more glad to see the twin white cups of a telephone on the side of the house and the wires running across the garden, above a neglected mass of old lilac and apple trees, in the clear moon. At first sight it did not seem to be a very large house; he was deceived by the flat brick front, by what was really a large hooded doorway that through long years had become dwarfed to a mere hole under a drab arch of dusty ivy. It was only later that he discovered that its frontal narrowness concealed a house that seemed to stretch back without ending; as if successive owners had been shamed by the flat funereal front into adding piece after piece behind, until the final glassy crown had been achieved by putting on a large hexagonal conservatory at the back.

She came to the door with a book in her hand and wearing a dressing gown. At least, that first time, he had the idea that it was a dressing gown. Afterwards he saw her once more in the same garment, in better light, and he realized then that it was a dark blue woollen dress, old-fashioned, waistless, tied about the middle with a cord. She continually played with this cord, making motions of tying and untying it, without achieving any change in it at all.

He apologized and raised his cap to her and asked if he might use the telephone.

"What is the matter?" she said.

"My truck," he said. "I blew a gasket. I want to get a garage —"

"There's no telephone here," she said.

He said something about the wires going across the garden but she said:

"I had it cut off. There wasn't much use for it. Nobody called much." And then: "There's a box half a mile down the road."

He said thank you and how sorry he was for disturbing her at that time of night and asked which way the box was.

"It's on the corner of the little road. The one on the left you passed a little way back." Up to that moment she had been framed with an almost faceless obscurity under the canopy of ivy, against a background of a single electric bulb of meager wattage that seemed to bathe the hall and staircase behind her in a kind of smoky orange varnish. Now she came out into the moonlight and said:

"I'll just show you. Where's your truck? Where are you from?"

"London," he said and he found she was looking with a sort of microscopic, eager curiosity, almost queerly, up into his face.

"London," she said. "You drive all that way? This time of night?"

"Three nights a week," he said.

"Where do you sleep?"

"Sleep before I start," he said. "I get five minutes' doss sometimes in the cab —"

He still could not see her face very clearly in the moonlight and now he discovered it was for two reasons. She had a habit of walking with her head down, as if she was fascinated by her hands playing with such restless indetermination with the cord of her dress. Her face too was three parts obscured by a frame of thick black hair. Afterwards he saw her hair in that particular fashion, like the dress, only once more, but that first night it gave him an impression of untidy, uneasy strength, so that he found himself suddenly glad that the telephone box was down the road.

Then she said: "Does it mean your truck is stranded? Can't you go any farther? How much farther have you to go?"

"About a hundred and fifty," he said.

She seemed to consider this and once again he found her looking at him with microscopic inquisitiveness, from eyes that were simply two dark holes under the drawn-down frame of hair. Then suddenly she said:

"You can use the telephone if you like. That wasn't true what I said about being cut off. But I didn't know who you were — you've got to be careful, haven't you? But I can see you're all right now — you're a nice fellow. I can see that."

"Thanks all the same. I won't bother you. I'll hop down the road."

"No, no," she said. "Oh, no! Don't do that. It's a long

way. Don't do that. Come in now. You can use the telephone. I've got some tea going. I always have tea going at
this time. I drink tea all night."

He thought for a moment that she was going to pull
him by the hand. Her own hand seemed to snatch at the
moonlight in a hungry sort of gesture, almost a pounce,
not unlike the grab that a child might make, too late, at a
butterfly.

"You could ring up the Acme Service," she said.
"They'll come out. They're four miles down the road.
Then you can have some tea while you're waiting."

He thanked her and said all right, he would, and he
followed her into the house. The telephone, an old-fashioned fixed wall model, was in the hall, under the single
small electric bulb, and while he was telephoning he
could smell the fumes of a spirit kettle coming from a
room somewhere beyond.

The garage would be an hour, they said; they had only
one night-service breakdown truck and that was out.
When he heard this he remembered he still had his supper in a haversack in the cab.

"Where are you going?" she said.

"I've got a bit of food in the truck," he said. "I'll just
get it —"

"Oh, no! Don't bother with that. I've got food. If you're
hungry I have food."

So he followed her into the first of what he knew later

were many rooms beyond it. It was a large room, furnished in a sort of suburban Jacobean, with a heavy beamed ceiling, encrusted white wallpaper, a big paneled oak fireplace and a bulb-legged dining table in the center. In one corner was a divan covered by a blue and purple paisley shawl. She sat untidily, almost sloppily, on this divan, in the light of a small brass table-lamp and the mauve flames of the spirit kettle, and told him that that was where she slept.

"That's when I do sleep," she said. "I don't sleep much. I'm like you — awake most of the night. I have tea and read and then drop off when it's day."

He saw that the spirit kettle was silver, like the big teapot she presently filled with water. The cups were of thin china, fancily flowered, with high handles.

"I hear the trucks go by all night," she said. "It's funny — I expect I've heard you go by many a time. What's your name? Mine's Broderick. Mrs. Broderick."

"Charlie," he said. "Charlie Williams."

"Like the prince, eh?" she said.

Now, in the double light of the lamp and the spirit kettle, he could see her face more clearly. It was a very white face, the kind of face molded by sleepless nights and airless days into a mask of paste that made it difficult for him to tell how old she was. He noticed she did not smile. Once or twice it occurred to him that she was a woman of fifty or so, and then suddenly her head would turn sideways in the mauve and yellow glow of light. The profile, no longer depressed by the huge black bunch of hair, became delicate, the line of the pale lips unexpectedly much younger.

All this time she was lighting one cigarette after another: lighting it, putting it down, forgetting it, lighting a second from the first and then forgetting again. In this distracted fashion it was some time before she remembered she had promised him some food.

"I'm sorry. What would you like? Meat or something? Some cheese?"

"Cheese," he said, "thank you."

She went away and came back after some moments with the bone of a leg of lamb and a loaf of bread and a big bone-handled carving knife. She held the bone in one hand and sliced off chunks of meat with the other and laid them between pieces of bread.

"You remind me of somebody," she said. "I've got an idea I've seen you before."

"Perhaps going by in the truck," he said.

"No," she said, "it couldn't be that."

She seemed to lapse into a momentary coma of thought, disturbed, stubbing her cigarette absently into a saucer, her head down.

"Tell me about yourself," she said. "I know you live in London and you come by three nights a week. What else? Where do you live?"

"Paddington."

"Married?"

"No," he said. "Not me."

"Not you?" she said. "A young fellow like you?"

"Pick 'em up and lay 'em down," he said, "that's me for the moment. I don't want to get tied up. Who wants a night driver anyway? They want you home and in bed."

She laughed for the first time. Her voice had been pitched rather low, much as if she had become fixed in the habit of talking to herself, but the laugh was several notes higher, lifting, rather delicate, a pleasant singing spring of relief.

"You make me laugh," she said.

She turned up the flame of the spirit kettle and then poured more water on the tea. She filled his cup and her own again and said:

"When will you be going back?"

"Ought to be going back tomorrow," he said. "Depends on the gasket."

"It's funny about people," she said. "You coming by here hundreds of times and then you suddenly have trouble and come in and here we are talking."

It was after midnight when the breakdown truck arrived. As he walked out into the road with the driver he had an impression that she was coming too, but when he turned she had gone from the doorway and back into the house.

It was while he and the driver were still fixing the tow chain that he heard her coming across the road. She was running with light, almost palpitating steps and she had a vacuum flask and a paper parcel in her hands.

"I almost thought I wouldn't catch you," she said. "It's just a flask of tea and the lamb bone. You can have it at the garage while you wait. I saw how you tucked into the lamb —"

"That's kind of you," he said.

"Not a bit. You can bring the flask back when you come by again. I'd be glad of it back."

She stood in the road, huddled, thoughtful, watching the two of them hitching the tow chain, for about ten minutes longer. Her face was dead white in the moon. When the chain was fixed and just before he got up into the cab he thanked her again and said good night. She lifted a thin arm in farewell and at the same moment he heard from the direction of the house a man's voice calling, in a snapped, thin screech, what he afterwards knew was her Christian name:

"Francie! Francie! For heaven's sake where are you? Francie!"

And as if it had nothing to do with her or she had not heard it or did not care if she heard it she stood impassively by the trucks and said to him up in the cab:

"Don't forget the flask, will you? I shall be here."

Before he could speak the voice screeched for her

again but she still stood there, unmoved, in impassive in-
difference, waiting for the trucks to go. He called down
that he would not forget the flask. In that moment he saw
her smile again and that was how he came to see her for
the second time.

She must have thought that he was coming back by
night. But the garage was small, the size he wanted in
gaskets was not in stock, and it was well past breakfast
time before he was on the road again. In that way, instead of coming back by night, he was driving through
the long switchbacks of low chalk hillsides soon after noon
the following day.

Stopping the truck by the house, getting down with the
flask in his hand, looking at the ugly deceptive brick front
half lost in its scabby broken apple tree, he did not attach
much importance to it all. He had had kindnesses on the
road from women before and he had often given kindnesses, in the way truck drivers do, to people in trouble
or cars that had broken down, and sometimes women had
slipped a note in his hand. There had been a time, once,
in Wiltshire, on a late summer evening, when he had
helped an old woman get back a charging sow into a sty.
The old woman was weeping; she kept saying that her
old man would knock her brains out when he came back
from the pub and found she had let the pig loose; but he
comforted her and she too, like the others, gave him tea.

She even promised him a cut of the bacon when the pig was killed and cured, but he had never bothered to go back and claim it. When you traveled about so much, especially at night, you came up against some odd capers.

It had been rather warm for April that afternoon and with the sun full on the glass of the cab he had been glad to drive in his shirt sleeves. He felt cheerful in the sun; already he was beginning to feel that he could look forward to the warmer, easier nights of summertime.

The bell on the front door was one of those old-fashioned iron pulls that connect far back into the house, and he pulled at it several times before he realized that it was no longer working. He tried the front door gently but it was locked and he was thinking of leaving the vacuum flask in the porch when he thought he heard sounds from the back of the house.

That was how he first discovered how far back the house extended. Bit by bit, bay by bay, its owners had grotesquely enlarged it, trying to cover, and at the same time always increasing, its original hideousness. On one side a tower, a red-brick pepper box with terra-cotta sills and facings, had been built, and above it was a flagpole. Beyond it was a wing that seemed insecure in its attachment to the rest of the house and that someone had fortified with four stout stone buttresses.

And then, at the extreme back, behind another shrubbery of lilac and rose and flowering currant, all deep in

the witherings of last summer's grasses, he came upon the
conservatory. It was hexagonal in shape and its upper
windows were panes of colored glass, deep blue, green,
yellow, bright blood-red. And to his astonishment it was
full of flowers.

He did not know much about flowers but as he pushed
open the door the scent of them from the steamy interior
poured out at him with powerful intoxication. That afternoon the inside temperature of the house must have been
a hundred degrees; he could actually see steam rising from
rows of pipes under the banks of staged flowers. He did
not know the names of a single one of these flowers; he
was simply stupefied, for the next few seconds, by the
mass of exotic blossom rising from banks of dripping fern.

That was only the beginning of his astonishment. Some
seconds later he was aware of being looked at. What
seemed to be a face sprinkled, flower-fashion, with splashes
and blobs of blue and crimson and yellow and green
was staring at him from under the rim of a pale straw
hat.

This small figure resolved itself presently into that of
a man in a biscuit-colored alpaca jacket, a narrow starched
collar and black pin-stripe trousers. The fact that he wore
no necktie gave a seminaked, half-finished appearance to
what was otherwise a dapper little body that sat with a
kind of doll-like erectness in a wicker chair. The face
would have been deep yellow under the sparse white

hair if it had not been blobbed with scraps of reflection from the colored panes in the roof above. It was these blotches of mingled blue and crimson and yellow and green that gave it an unhealthy appearance, the total unreality of a curious, bright disease.

For some seconds the figure did not move. It seemed torpid in the hot and steamy air. The lids of the eyes were exactly like those of a frog flabbily sunk in stupor.

Then Williams saw them shoot into squinty wakefulness, and the voice that screeched at him was the voice he had already heard, once before, calling the woman Francie.

"Get out," it said.

"O.K.," Williams said, "no harm. I was just looking for Mrs. Broderick to give her the tea flask back."

"Mrs. Broderick is not here. Get out."

"All right, guvnor, all right."

"And to bring the what back?"

"The tea flask. That's all. It doesn't matter though. I can leave it here —"

"Where did you get that thing?"

"She lent it me. The other night. I busted a gasket and she give me some tea."

"Get out!" he screeched. "I don't like people roaming about here. I don't like louts in here."

"Louts?"

Up to that moment Williams had been patient, unruffled, a little amused. Now he felt the personal affront, the whip of the word louts, go ripping him with anger. The small figure in the chair suddenly looked to him like a dressed-up maggot. It reminded him powerfully of one of those advertisements for pest-killers in which grub and caterpillar sit up on their hind legs with expressions of sinister greed among the flowers they live to destroy. He felt his big arms twitch as he looked at it. He felt that with one single twist of them he could have rubbed it out. There would have been a little mess on the wet, steaming bricks between the stagings of bright flowers and then it would all have been over.

Then he calmed; his sense of humor came back.

"Look here, grandad, don't you call me lout. I don't like it, see? See that, grandad? I don't like it."

In a moment his impression of looking at a dressed-up maggot was gone. His vision cleared. He saw before him once again nothing but the bloodless torpid little figure, pathetic and somehow spurious in the straw hat.

"You want to git out in the fresh air, grandad," he said. "It ain't healthy in here. You git hot under the collar —"

"Get out!" The screech, this time, was several times louder than before. It set the mouth blubbering with a series of foaming convulsions. "You cheap lout! Get out of here!"

A moment later Williams caught himself in the act of

throwing the vacuum flask. He actually had it poised above his head. At the word cheap all his rage came rushing back.

"You call me cheap just once more, grandad, and I'll lay you among the daisies —"

He did not know quite what he was ready to do at that moment. Once more he could see the maggot in the chair; once more he was aware of the ease with which he could rub it out.

It was her voice which stopped all this:

"Good afternoon," she said. He turned to see her standing behind him, in the blue old-fashioned dress: gray-eyed, pale, calm, almost phlegmatic, her appearance, as he thought, somewhere between a governess and a housekeeper who had come in time to stop a bout of rowdiness between two boys.

"I beg pardon, Mrs. Broderick," Williams said. "I just came to return the tea flask. Only I don't think grandad likes me." His humor, dry and sprightly, was already back. "Don't like my face or something, do you, grandad?"

He turned as he said this and he saw that the chair was empty. And all at once he felt himself tricked by an illusion that it had never been occupied. The maggot was a myth; the straw hat, the torpid-eyed creature sitting among the sweltering forest of fern and flower had never been.

"Where's grandad?" He was laughing wryly. "Must have slipped down a hole or something —"

"I'm sorry he annoyed you."

She paused and was looking at him again with gray microscopic curiosity. "Don't let him do it again. Just stop him. Be hard with him. It's the only way. It's just his childishness."

It had been too dark to notice the color of her eyes before. Now he saw how brilliant and startling their grayness was. He saw also that his impression of a woman of fifty or so was quite ridiculous. In the bright afternoon light she was clearly not more than forty. And if the thick black hair had drooped less about her face and the blue woolen dress less about the figure he might even have given her, he thought, the benefit of thirty-five.

"I thought you would come last night," she said.

He explained how he had not been able to make it earlier.

"I had the tea made. I waited. I suppose a hundred trucks must have gone by."

"Well, thank you for the flask," he said. "I got to push on."

"Oh, no!" she said. "I've got some tea made. Just a cup. And there's something I want to ask you. Oh, it won't take a moment — you can spare a moment, can't you?"

She smiled; the gray eyes were steeped in a brilliant mist of persuasion, not very obvious or insistent, but so positive that it did not enter his head to do anything else but follow her into the house.

The tea, as she said, was already made, but this time in a big brown homely sort of pot. "I know you like it strong," she said. "You drivers always do." She carved him from a large square block a slice of heavy fruit cake. "And you like that too, I know."

He did not know quite what to say to this easy and friendly attention and he started talking, as people mostly do, of the weather.

"It's turned out a nice day," he said. "Like summer in the cab."

"Oh, has it?" she said. "I hadn't noticed. I'm always asleep in the daytime. Or half asleep. Besides it always rains here, across the hills. This is where the cloud breaks."

For the next few minutes, as he drank a second cup of tea and ate a second piece of cake, he kept thinking of the little man in the conservatory. He was puzzled about the torpid grublike figure crowned by the straw hat. He was mystified by its sudden disappearance out of the forest of flowers. He wanted to ask about it and did not know how to frame his question. Instead he said:

"You were going to ask me something, weren't you?"

"When you've finished your tea," she said. "Another cup? Another piece of cake?"

He thanked her and said no, it was really time he got

on. The gray eyes were fixed on his forearms, where the
light brown hairs were almost sandy against the muscular
flesh still white from winter.

He suddenly felt slightly self-conscious about this gaze
and got up. What was it she was going to ask him? he
said.

"You won't think I'm imposing on you, will you?" she
said. Now she too was standing up. She was fairly tall, so
that her face was level with his own. "You won't, will
you?" She was smiling; the gray eyes were pleasantly pel-
lucid, mercurial, with soft light. "I feel it awful cheek, I
know it is — but would you do a little errand in London?"

"Well, sure if I can."

"It's just a note about a dress," she said.

She had an envelope in her hands.

"If you would just take this note to this address they
will give you the dress and then perhaps you could bring
it back next time you come down? Could you?" She
smiled again and gave a relieved sort of sigh. "I feel so
ashamed about asking you."

It crossed his mind that it was odd she could not post
her envelope, but she seemed ready for that:

"The last time they sent a dress down the box broke
open and there was a fruit stain on it. I could never
wear it. I could never get it out."

She saw him looking at the address on the envelope
and said:

"Oh, yes, it's off Wigmore Street. It isn't a stone's throw from you. I've told them who you are in the note and it will be all right. Are you sure you don't mind?"

"Not a bit."

"I'm so glad. When will you be back?"

"Day after tomorrow."

"At night?"

"At night," he said. "About eleven."

She came out with him as far as the truck. The sun was hot on the white chalk road. Sprigs of apple blossom were breaking on the old scabby trees; the crest of every hedgerow was sprinkled with the bright lace of new leaves.

"Good-by," she said. She waited for him to climb up into the cab. "It's most awfully kind of you to do that for me."

Something, at the last moment, made him feel that he was entitled to a gesture in return.

"By the way," he said, "who was grandad? He didn't seem to like me."

Obliquely she looked past him, as if troubled by sun.

"That's Calvin," she said. "That's my husband."

The motor was running; he let in the clutch smoothly. She stood in the road, watching him with a face that was negative, with gray eyes that were still so unstirred and so incalculable that they were almost without identity.

"At least what's left of him," she said. "But take no notice of that."

After that he began to stop at the house every time he went down and every time he came back again. At first she provided the excuses to stop. And they seemed, he thought, like casual excuses. There was a dress to be brought down from London, another to be taken back. She was short of tea once and he bought a small chest for her in Yeovil as he came up from the West. Through the nights when she did not sleep she did a great deal of reading and now and then he would collect a parcel of books for her in London. Once or twice there was change from the money she gave him for these things and each time she said:

"No, you keep that. That's for you. Buy yourself a drink with that."

Then, after a week or two, there was no need for the invention of excuses. It became a simple and congenial habit to stop by the craggy blossoming apple trees, whose scent he could smell in the warm wet May darkness. It became something to look forward to: tea, a meat sandwich, a hunk of fruit cake, a rest in the dark subdued house, in the mauve light of the spirit flames, perhaps a wash after the oily hot drive down.

And perhaps because it was now always night when he saw her he did not, for a week or two, notice any change

in her. But presently the days were almost fully length-
ened; the evenings began to be white with midsummer.
And on an evening in early June, after a long bright day,
the light had still not faded when he parked the truck.

That evening the front door of the house was open but
she was not lying down, as she nearly always was, on the
paisley-shawled divan in the big front room. The spirit
lamp was not burning. The room was still quite full of
light.

While he waited he walked about the room, looking at
many photographs of her that stood on tables and shelves
and the big oak mantelpiece. There were perhaps a dozen
or fifteen of these pictures of her and he had never really
noticed them before.

He was still looking at them when she came in. She
said something about Calvin being naughty, Calvin
playing up, and how tiresome it all was. "He is getting so
that he has a taste for the barbitone," she said. "Just a
craving. Like people do for whisky. He used to sleep well
with one or two. Now it's three or four or five."

She had been quick to notice that he had been looking
at the photographs and now she said:

"Oh, don't look at those awful pictures of me! They're
deadly. I ought to hide them up."

"I thought they were very nice," he said.

"Oh! You did? Which one did you like best?"

More at random than anything he picked on one in

which she was wearing a white blouse and rather tight-fitting black skirt; the blouse had a square neck, rather low, across which there was a strip of lace insertion. Her dark hair was piled rather lightly and her figure, under the smooth white blouse, was thrown rather high up, so that she looked full-fleshed and assertive and strikingly young.

"Why that one?" she said. "Why do you like that one?"

"I don't know," he said. "I just do —"

"I'm glad you like that one. Do you know why?"

He said no, he couldn't think why.

"Because it's the last one taken before I was married," she said. "Ten years ago. Seems like a lifetime."

The room was still quite light and perhaps he turned instinctively to see if the woman he had known for only four or five weeks could possibly be the same person as the girl in the picture. He was at once arrested by some odd quality of change in her; she seemed to have become, for some reason, uncannily like the younger girl. There was an air of something fresher about her face and his apparent difficulty about accounting for this seemed to amuse her.

"You see something different in me?" She was smiling, showing her teeth.

"I think there is something different," he said.

"Don't you know what it is?"

No: in his obtuse, clumsy, masculine way he did not know what it was.

She gave her body a full turn, suddenly, and then said:

"It's my hair. Didn't you notice? I'm doing it in the old way."

His surprise at his own stupidity at not noticing how her hair was now piled high again, achieving an effect of lightness and freshness in her entire face, must have been responsible for his giving a gasp of pleasure.

"You like it, do you?" she said.

"Yes."

"I hoped you would. I went down today and had it done. You know why today?"

He had not the slightest idea about that either. The circumstances had the effect, altogether, of bewitching him a little and he could only stare.

"Because it's my birthday," she said. "At least it will be at twelve o'clock. Did you bring the dress?"

"Yes, I got it."

"That's for my birthday too. I treated myself."

The dress was in its box on a chair. She untied the string and parted the tissue wrappings and said, "Emerald. Do you think emerald will suit me? You don't think green is unlucky, do you?"

She took out the dress and held it in front of her, pinning it to her shoulders with the points of her fingers. The

light was fading by that time and the color of the dress
was a sharp strong green.

"Well, say if you like it."

Yes, he liked it, he said. He was still feeling the effects
of a sense of slight bewitchment and he hardly heard her
say:

"Shall I put it on? I was going to put it on for the party
anyway." He could not conceive what she meant by a
party but she went on: "A party for me. Tonight — just
you and me. That's if you'll stay. You don't mind if I slip
it on here, do you? It's nearly dark now —"

She began to slip off the dress she was wearing, the old
blue woolen dress that he had seen several times before,
and then she put the new dress quickly over her head and
shoulders. In her haste she forgot to undo the clips at the
neck, so that she had to take it off and begin again. Something about this repeated upward stretch of her white
arms in the darkening room turned his sense of bewitchment into a final moment of distraction. In another moment he was holding her by the soft upper part of her
arms. His blood was beating heavily through him and she
was reaching up to him with her mouth.

She found it hungrily; and then, when he had kissed
her for that first time, she had only one thing to say.

"I began to think," she said, "that you'd never notice
me."

He had not intended to go as far as that; he had never

had any thought that it would be more than a casual episode. The situation took him by surprise. It was another pick 'em up and lay 'em down affair and he could not resist its distraction.

But that night, after what she called her party, he was not so much aware of the pleasant nature of her body as the insistence of her voice, suddenly freed, emotionally charged, talking on into the morning, disjointedly, telling him about herself, about Calvin, her marriage and how she had come there and what a dreary bore it was.

The party had consisted of a bottle of gin, a pile of thick ham sandwiches which she had tried in vain, in a bungling way, to make elegant by removing the crusts, and a large white sugary cake, her birthday cake, made by herself and inscribed with her own best wishes: *Lisa: a Happy Birthday.*

He was puzzled by this inscription.

"I thought your name was Francie," he said.

"So it is," she said. "But Lisa — that's my pet name. It's a name somebody used to call me."

"Old flame?"

"In a way," she said, "yes. We went to a play together once and there was a girl in it named Lisa. You know how people are. Perhaps he saw something in her that was like me."

Anyway, she said, she didn't want to talk about that. Her hands groped for him in the half darkness. Where was he? she said. He seemed so far away. Then her mouth found his face again and she said:

"That's better than any talking, isn't it? Don't you like that better?"

Then, some time later, he was saying:

"That fellow. The one you went to the play with. Was he the one you thought I was like?"

"Partly," she said. "But you're bigger. You're a bigger man altogether —"

"What made you marry this one?" he said.

"Calvin?" Her voice, he remembered long afterwards, was surprisingly casual. It seemed, he thought, almost off-hand. "Oh, the usual — sort of rebound."

"From the other one?"

"He was killed," she said. Emotionlessly she spoke of the war, a raid somewhere, a bomb that with impersonal lack of drama had wiped a man out. "He went into a cinema somewhere and never came out again. There was nothing left. We were going to be married. I was going to have someone all to myself, and then —"

She laughed with a sort of dry stutter, almost a cough.

"And now here I am. Stuck," she said. "At first I came as housekeeper. Then he wanted to marry me." Her voice was flat. "Like that it was cheaper. He didn't have to pay me."

He said it occurred to him, not for the first time, that a simple solution would be to pack her bags and walk out.

Again she gave the short laugh that was between a cough and a stutter.

"Walk out? On about four hundred thousand?"

Before he had time to do anything about expressing his astonishment she asked him if he had ever heard of the Fresco Patent Clip Spring? She hadn't more than a vague idea what it was herself. It had something to do with time fuses, she thought.

"I think it's fuses," she said. "Something to do with the way a bomb goes off or a gun fires. I've never even seen one. But Calvin invented it. He draws a royalty on it until the end of time."

Thoughtfully he considered his picture of the little figure in the straw hat, the torpid angry maggot among the flowers.

"It wouldn't be bad, would it, four hundred thousand?" she said.

Her way of saying this too was casual. He could not even determine whether she was really addressing him or not. They were lying together on the shawl-covered divan. He could feel her body pressing against him in the darkness, and himself the central core of a quietness that was as unreal as her voice going on to frame her thoughts:

"What would you do with that much money if you had it? With even half of it? You know what I'd do? What I'm going to do? I'll have a house on an island somewhere where the sea's warm, where I can swim all day and lie in the sun. How's that, do you think? After years in a dump like this."

"How do you know you'll get this money?"

"I've seen the will," she said. "I know. It's in my favor. There isn't anyone else except me. And besides, he's fond of me. He likes me."

Walk out, his mind began saying, walk out. Before it's too late. Before you're in any deeper. Don't be a fool. And all the time he knew that he was a fool to be lying there with her, a woman of that particular sort of temperament, with a husband somewhere upstairs, and he turned involuntarily at the sound of a bough scratching the wall of the house outside.

"Lie still," she said. "There's nothing to be worried about."

Worried? he thought. Why should he be worried by the wizened maggoty little figure of grandad? Worried by grandad? That made him laugh.

"What are you laughing at?" she said.

Something made him say: "Me on an island. I was thinking of that. Nothing to do but lie in the sun all day. Swim and lie in the sun. What a caper."

He laughed again, amused by the sheer fantasy of it.

"What's funny about it?" she said.

"I'm a night driver. I drive a two-ton truck."

"You're twenty-five," she said. "Is that what you want

to do all your life? Drive a truck? Slog up and down here?"

Was it what he wanted? No, he supposed it wasn't. He hadn't thought about it. He must always have supposed it was what he wanted. He'd got used to it. It wasn't bad.

Before he could speak she stirred in the darkness. She raised herself on one elbow and leaned over him, brushing her mouth against his face with a surprising, delicate tenderness and the curve of her body against his own.

"It's nearly daylight," she said. "You must love me and leave me. You're hours behind."

"I'll make it up."

He lay still on the divan, resting the back of his head on his hands.

"Don't you want to go?" she said. "Do you like it with me? Do I make it so nice for you?"

"I wouldn't call it bad."

She laughed quietly, kissing him again.

"I wish I was coming with you. A free day and a long ride — just you and me in the truck. That would be nice, wouldn't it? But perhaps some day I will ride with you — what do you think? When I get out of this?"

"But not in a truck."

"No, not in a truck," she said.

When she came out to see him drive away she had her birthday cake wrapped up for him in a box.

"It seems funny, doesn't it?" she said. "Having to make your own birthday cake and put your name on it and give it to yourself? If it hadn't been for you I wouldn't have known I had a birthday."

For the first time she seemed to speak with bitterness; she seemed to gasp in suppression of a sob. He felt all at once affectionately sorry for her. He thought how touching and nice she looked standing there, in the growing daylight, below his driving cab, in the new emerald dress.

"That's how I live," she said. "I might as well be a widow on a shoestring."

In a sudden effort to cheer her up he winked.

"See you tomorrow, Lisa."

The gray eyes seemed to draw slightly together as they smiled, like two bright steel points closing together to hold him there.

"I love you for saying that," she said.

It was three weeks later when he drove up, late one night, in a raging thunderstorm. The August air was heavy with the stifling vapor of nearly a day of hot and steaming rain. In the big numerous flashes of lightning he could see whole fields of wheat and barley lying flattened as white straw mats under a dripping sky. And as the weight of his truck hit the floods of water the road in front of him kept exploding in white water spouts, like the echoes of thunder.

He had never been so glad of the thought of her as he was that night. His clothes were drenched with sweat and most of the time his thought was of a dry room, tea, something to eat, a chance to lie down in quietness with her, out of the harsh dazzle of his headlights on the streaming windscreen in the humid darkness and rain.

But the moment he saw her he knew that there was no chance of quietness. Instead of the usual lamp by the divan, together with the blue flame of the spirit kettle, he saw that the big heavy Jacobean chandelier was full on. She was walking up and down underneath it, smoking a cigarette, pulling hard at it in agitation. On the table was a full ash tray of cigarette stubs. The front of her dress was dusty with ash and for the first time since he had seen her, on the night he had blown the gasket, he thought she looked untidy and old and tired.

She was so agitated that she made no attempt to kiss him. In fact in a queer way he had an idea that she resented his presence there.

"I didn't think you'd turn up in this," she said.

He said something about having to try to make it whatever the weather was, but he had an impression that she neither heard nor cared what he said. Some of the time he had been thinking of her idea of an island in sunshine. "Somewhere out of this blasted rain. Out of this God-forsaken climate," he had been thinking. "Anything to get out of this."

And now, almost as if she knew he had been thinking exactly that, she said:

"I think Calvin is on his way out. I think he might even be dead. I daren't go up to him."

He said "God," very quietly, under his breath. Through his mind went a reminder, jolting, preposterous, a little sickening, of the four hundred thousand she had spoken about and he said unsteadily:

"What makes you think that? What's the matter with him?"

"It's the dud heart," she said. "And the thundery weather. He can't get his breath in this weather."

"I better push on," he said.

"No, don't go," she said. "We've got to find out if he's all right before you go."

We? he thought and a first sensation of wild uneasiness shot through him like a palpitation.

"He always has a glass of whisky about nine and then two or three tablets. That puts him off generally," she said.

"Has he had them yet?"

"Not yet," she said. "I went up at six and he was lying there like a stone. I haven't been up since. I daren't go up. He was lying there like a stone."

"Must have been asleep."

"It didn't look like sleep. It looked queer. Different from sleep," she said.

He did not know quite how he walked up the wide carpetless oak stairs. His shoes were so noisy that he felt a horrible and compelling notion that he ought to take them off in deference to the possible dead lying there somewhere in the rooms above him. At the last moment she had reminded him to take the whisky bottle and a glass, but he had even forgotten to ask her which room, and then suddenly she called up to him from below:

"You'll see it. The room at the end of the corridor. There's a light. There's always a light there."

He felt he ceased, in that moment, to be himself. It was exactly as if he had taken his shoes off and was walking under the compulsion of a series of muffled reflexes. And before he really knew it he was in the bedroom.

It was a big bedroom and in the center of it, not pushed back against the wall, was a cheap brass bed. The floor was covered with linoleum and a single night light in a saucer was burning on a table beside the bed. On the west wall of the room a high sash window had been left open and rain was pouring in on the linoleum, which shone like gray wet skin in the flashes of lightning.

"Mr. Broderick," he said quietly, "Mr. Broderick."

There was to be one more occasion after that when he was to stand there before the little bloodless figure and say the same words and wait with breathless, still more terribly anxious tension for an answer. This first time there was no answer. All his own breathing seemed to have stopped by that time and all he could hear in return for his third mention of Broderick's name was the stiff croak of a throat slowly gasping, like the dry gyrations of some old unoiled machine, for breath.

Then he saw Broderick sitting up, dummy-wise, hands stiff and outstretched, in the bed. He did not know whether it was pure relief or vexation or fright about something that made him stride across the room and shut the window. The edges of its frame were so wet that his hands slipped as he grasped it and it came down with a crack on the flooded sill. Rain was still coming down heavily but the storm was veering away now and the flashes of lightning were simply like far-off stabbing light-echoes on the hills.

"Mrs. Broderick sent me up to shut the window," he said.

That seemed as good an excuse as any, he thought, to offer to the figure that had not moved an inch in the bed since he had opened the door. Now he went a few paces nearer the bed and said:

"All right, grandad? Why don't you go to sleep now?"

He rubbed the sweaty palms of his hands down the sides of his trouser legs and began to feel better as he saw, in the glow of the night light, the little eyes responding with dumb delicacy to his stare.

"You remember me, don't you, grandad?" Again there

was no answer. "Why don't you be a good boy, grandad, and have your whisky and drop off for a while?"

He was quite near the bed now. The sound of Broderick gasping for breath reminded him of the croak of the sheep he sometimes heard when he stopped his truck in some remote still place in the dead of nighttime.

And suddenly, inexplicably, again perhaps out of pure relief, he felt sorry for him. There was something appalling and touching about the little erect dummy sitting there in half darkness, in mute paralysis, in the sound of thunder and driving rain, like a child frightened by a storm.

Something made him put out his hands and touch the hands that lay outstretched on the bed. The contact of their scabby frigid flesh was something he never forgot. He felt he was touching death in living flesh and only once again, afterwards, was he so repulsed and so frightened.

"Come on, grandad," he said. He took the unresisting, terribly light shell of bone and skin in his hands and tried to make it, very gently, lie back on the pillow.

"Where is Francie?" it said.

"She's tired. She's having a lay-down. She's tired out worrying about you."

"She's a good girl, Francie," he said. "It's not much fun for her here."

That too, Williams found, was surprisingly touching. He had always suspected something in the nature of a feud between them: one of those dreary drawn-out feuds that each side knows only death can extirpate. Now his surprise was all the greater, not only because there was affection there, on the part of the old man at any rate, but because Broderick suddenly said:

"You're a truck driver, aren't you? She told me how kind you'd been to her."

"Ah, that's all right," he said. "Like to help people if I can."

"Do you? She's been very kind to me. Very kind. For a long time. She deserves a little herself."

"What about having your tablets now, grandad, and dropping off for a bit?"

"I can't sleep with this weather," Broderick said. "I can't get my breath."

"You have your tablets and a drop of whisky and you'll sleep like a cat," he said.

"Whisky?"

"Whisky — yes. I brought it up," Williams said. "It's over on the chest of drawers here."

"Who said I could have whisky? I am not supposed to have whisky. For several years I've not had whisky. I used to be very fond of it —"

"Ah, come on, you can have whisky. You know you can have whisky. Mrs. Broderick says you can."

"I used to have it — a year or two back, but —"

"You have a tot, grandad," he said. "It'll do you good."

He poured a fair measure of whisky into a glass and one of his clearest images of Broderick that night was of the little quivering figure sitting up in bed with a strange grin on its face in the glow of the night light. It was the sunny, bright-eyed grin of a boy who had been bribed by sweetness or promises to lie down and be good and go to sleep at last. With loud relish the old dry mouth sucked and lapped at the whisky as Williams said:

"How many tablets?"

"I've been taking three or four."

"All right. Say four."

Just before they said good night Williams picked up the whisky bottle and said, "All right now, grandad? Think you can get off now?" and he saw the old eyes, already waked from their torpor by the excitement of liquor, regarding him and the bottle with keen, bright greed.

"Now, grandad, don't tell me you want a refill already. You on the wagon all this time too."

"Just a thimbleful."

As Williams filled up the glass the hands quivered with a start of greedy joy.

"What about you?" Broderick said. "A drop for you?"

He said something about it being late and there not being another glass, but Broderick pointed to the bottle. There was actually the crease of a smile on his face as he did so. Williams picked up the bottle and took a deep steady gulp of whisky and Broderick said:

"At one time the doctors used to say it would kill me. Why don't you sit down a minute with me?"

"Better not, grandad. Got to push on."

"Where are you going? You're the night driver, aren't you? She told me about you."

"Other side of Exeter. Get there by breakfast time."

"I see. It's very nice of you to stop with me. How do you find the whisky? I prefer it neat, don't you?"

All this was said slowly, with croaking difficulty, between crackling gasps for breath. In spite of it all the crease of a smile actually reappeared once or twice again. Finally he made another gesture or two towards the whisky bottle and one more towards his glass.

"No more, grandad. Got to drive, y'know. You'll get me for the high jump, smelling like a four-ale bar."

"Well: all right. But you'll come in again, won't you?"

"Some time. Don't have much time, most nights."

"Please come in," Broderick said, and the crease of a smile, yellowish, more than ever like the crinkle in the neck of a pale maggot slowly turning its head, came back again. "I like to talk to you. Don't get much chance of talking."

As he went out of the room with its dim night light embalming and enshrining Broderick with its upward glow Williams felt the absence of death so keenly that he could do nothing but joke about it as a man jokes about an escape from it.

"Perky as a chicken," he said. Downstairs, in the hall, she was waiting for him exactly as he had left her, almost as if she might have been listening all that time. "Probably live to be a hundred."

"Don't talk like that," she said. Her face was an extraordinary sight in the poorish light of the one electric light bulb shining through its stained glass bowl above her. It seemed twisted with tension. The muscles of the neck and cheeks were sucked in, darkly, making her fiercely alert and cadaverous. "You mustn't talk like that. If you'd seen him this afternoon —"

And then suddenly:

"What about the whisky? Did you give him his whisky?"

"Whisky?" Williams laughed softly. "You should have seen us. Totting it out. The two of us. Having a good old buddies' party."

"I can't understand why you joke about it," she said.

And long afterwards, when it was all over, that was one of the things he could not understand himself. Only the blindest kind of a fool could have joked about it. But that night, in his relief that he had not had to deal with death, he was glad of it as something of a distraction to seize on. It was not really that he was joking about it; perhaps the whisky had pepped him up a bit, he thought. He was just relieved that death had not complicated things. He did not want to be mixed up with death. If there was anything he loathed and hated it was dying and the dead. He had once seen the body of a man on the roadside, just out of London, lying on the grass, after a smash, the face covered with a sheet of newspaper, and the sight of it leered backwards and forwards across his mind, grotesque and haunting, for nights and days.

"You'd better go now," she said.

When he took hold of her shoulders to say good night he found that she was shivering. The tendons of her neck were drawn and cold. If it had not been for the intense pressure of light burning in the eyes it might have been, in fact, that she was the person who had died.

"Here, come on. Come on," he said. "You got to pull yourself together. You got to snap out of this."

He heard her teeth crack against themselves, like a key snapping in a lock.

"I don't want to be alone here when it happens," she said. "That's all. I can't bear to be alone here with that."

"Don't get jittery," he said. "I'll be back tomorrow."

"All right," she said. She seemed to make a great effort to calm herself. She drew in a deep rasping breath. "You'll know by the blinds if anything has happened."

He supposed he must have called again five or six times, for perhaps ten days or so, perhaps two weeks, before two things occurred. Like so many other things that had happened, both were casual. Each time he repeated the habit of going upstairs and saying good night to Broderick — "Coming to tuck you up, grandad, and give you your nightcap" — seeing that the old crinkled neck swallowed its tablets, talking a little, sharing a glass of whisky with him, and it was after about the fourth or fifth of these visits that she said:

"You know, he's quite taken to you. He likes you. He told me so today. He quite looks forward to your coming."

And then, as if in an afterthought, more casually still:

"He told me something else about you."

"Bad, I'll bet."

"No. He's probably going to alter his will and leave you a little money, that's all."

"Stone the crows," he said.

"There," she said, "wouldn't that be nice?"

"Well, knock me down."

"Now you'll be able to have your own island, won't you?"

"Now why would he want to do that?" Williams said. "I'm nobody. He hardly knows me."

"He says you help him to go on living," she said. "You give him confidence, he says." She smiled. "Of course I may have helped a bit. Just a bit — for you."

Later, on the divan, before he left, she again drew out

of the half darkness, for only the second time for several weeks, the old, insidious dream of the island: the sun, the sea, the leisure, the way they could live together. "Like this," she said. "All the time. No more of this awful country. Where you can't get warm. Where it's always raining. And these awful winters."

"That's me," he said. "I can go for plenty of that."

"Perhaps it won't be long now."

"Oh! I can wait — I can wait till Doomsday for stuff like that."

"And how long do you think I've been waiting?" She was almost yelling at him now, in a curious forced undertone, hoarse in the darkness with anger and frustration. "I've been waiting ten years and it seems like ten thousand — how would you like to wait like that? No fun, no bed, no nothing. When I married him they said he wouldn't live a year — not six months. A cardiac complaint like that, they said — it can't live. One bit of overertion and he'll drop down and it's all over."

Her voice was rasping now with a tearless, suppressed rage. "But you see it's never the sick that die, is it? It's the healthy that drop down dead. The sick just go dragging on forever."

For a moment it seemed that she was going to break into uncontrolled weeping. He heard her mouth sucking air in an enormous sob. Then it stopped suddenly and she said:

"I'm sorry. I didn't mean to get worked up like that. I don't know what I'd have done without you."

He did not know quite what to say. He was distracted, not for the first time, by the emotional change of her voice. It almost mesmerized him and then she said:

"It was bad enough when there wasn't you. But now it's awful. I can't wait like that any more — I can't wait much longer."

Before he went that night he thought he heard Broderick calling from his bedroom. "Yes, perhaps it's him," she said. "He's been terribly restless. Would you go up? You could give him another tablet or two if he's still awake. And just a sip to calm him down."

Two days later it happened that a mate of his, a day driver named Davies, broke his wrist at the depot when a starting handle kicked. He had been going to drive a load of plasterboard to Bristol. And that was how Williams found himself driving out of London at eight o'clock in the morning instead of eight o'clock at night, in misty September rain that sprayed back on his windscreen in a greasy film that never wiped away.

Twenty miles out he decided to stop and wash his windscreen and have a plate of eggs and bacon and some tea at a shack where he sometimes breakfasted coming back to London from the West. While the eggs were cooking, the woman who kept the shack lent him the morning paper and he sat for some moments with elbows on the counter, reading it, casually wondering whether he should do a horse named Snow Flurry at 40-1 at Hurst Park that afternoon or be sensible and have something each way on the favorite at Worcester, Lorelei.

Then while he was still reading, the woman leaned over from behind the tea urn and said:

"There's a thing there that give me a turn when I got down this morning. Here, where is it, I was reading it when you come in. I'll see I never take another, if I lay awake a week. You see that?" she said. She turned the pages over for him. "My blessed fingers are all thumbs this morning. There — there it is."

Dully, not fully grasping it for a moment, he found himself reading the piece the woman had found for him. It was the account of the inquest on an actress who had died. Her death, the coroner said, was the third of its kind in a month: an alarming situation that should serve as a warning to people who took sleeping tablets and a nightcap of neat brandy or whisky on top. It could not be stated too strongly that the combination of these things was likely to be fatal.

"I done it," the woman said. "Two or three times last winter. And once last week. Two tablets and a tot of Johnny Walker. And neat at that. I hadn't slept right for a week. I felt I'd got to have something —"

The smell of eggs and bacon was suddenly an insufferable sickness, searing in his throat. A few moments later he was walking out of the shack, slopping through big black puddles of rain that lay all across the cinder surface of the pull-in.

For some time he did not know whether it was raining or not. It was perhaps ten or fifteen miles farther on that the clap-clack of windscreen wipers on dry glass really woke him. His hands were smeary with sweat and there was a dry acid crust on the walls of his throat. Most of the time he was not really seeing the road before him, drying in the September sun, but only the recurrent, entangled, haunting picture of the big ugly house that no one had ever seemed to stop building. It was a picture with something evil and luminous about it. He saw it in the purplish glow of the spirit kettle, then in the feeble aura of the night light and the broad stabbing flashes of lightning on the night he had first gone up to Broderick. He tried to remember how many times he had been up to that room and how many tablets and glasses he could have given Broderick and above all he kept thinking what a fool he had been ever to go there and stay there and listen to her.

The sun was hot in a clear noon sky by the time he came to within sight of the house. He decided to park the truck half a mile away, on the top of a hill, and walk the rest of the way to the back of the place. The air was humid and thick after rain and when he got out of his cab he felt his knees buckle and sag underneath him with complete absence of feeling that was more sickening than sudden pain.

He walked through a field at the back of the house and came into the garden through a fence that had fallen down under the weight of blackberry and bindweed. Instinctively he looked at the windows, but the blinds were not down. Up to that time he did not know quite what he was looking for. He was aware simply of groping in a scared cold way through sensations of nausea, through horror at being caught in a trap, through revulsion at the dead.

Then he remembered the conservatory. He remembered that that was where Broderick sat during most of the afternoon. He had heard her speak of a gardener named Smithson who came in for two hours in the morning to work among the flowers and then left at noon.

He did not know how long he stood in front of the conservatory door in exactly the way he had stood in the bedroom, in the storm, calling Broderick's name.

"Mr. Broderick," he said, "Mr. Broderick."

The little figure in the straw hat was sitting among the flowers. It seemed to be transfixed in the same torpid coma as when Williams had first seen it there. The skin of the face was blotched, as it had been then, with blobs of colored light streaming down, diffused, from the roof above, giving it the appearance of a marbled, artificial flower.

For a moment he could not make up his mind whether in fact he was not, after all, looking at the dead. All his sickness and revulsion came rushing back. Then he turned the handle of the door and through the steamy unreal heat of the conservatory he saw Broderick stir, raising his eyes from their torpor.

"Williams," Broderick said, "what are you doing here?"

Under the torrid glass, brilliant in the September afternoon sun, the bloodless face was actually bathed in sweat.

"Are you all right, Mr. Broderick?" Williams said. "I dropped in to see how you were."

"Perfectly all right." The face tottered in the overheated air like a petal about to fall. "This isn't your time, is it?"

"Got a change of job," Williams said. "I'm on day shift now. Are you sure you're all right, Mr. Broderick? Don't you want some air in here?"

"Perfectly all right," Broderick said. "Thanks to you." Incredulously Williams listened. In stupefaction he heard Broderick mumble on: "The whisky seems to have given me a new lease of life. Done me a power of good. Gives just enough stimulus to the heart without affecting it."

In the stifling heat, among the scent of flowers, Williams felt his own sweat prickling harshly through every pore.

"I got to go now, Mr. Broderick," he said. "Got to push on. Got to get down as far as Bristol before teatime."

"Haven't you seen Mrs. Broderick?"

"No."

"Don't you want to see her? I fancy she's asleep in the house somewhere."

"Not today," Williams said. "I got to push on today."

By that time he was standing by the door of the conservatory, holding it open, ready to go. Behind him the free cool air was blowing in.

"Shall I give her a message?" Broderick said. "Is there some message I can give?"

Message? For some moments he stood thinking that there was no message. He had nothing to say that made sense about an island, the sea, the sun or about Mrs. Broderick, who could not sleep at nighttime.

Then he decided, after all, that there was a message.

"Tell Mrs. Broderick," he said, "that I shan't be coming this way again." He was outside now; he was breathing at last the cool, sweet, free air. "Tell her that from now on I'll be working in the daytime."

Summer in Salandar

1

M ANSON lifted one corner of the green gauze window blind of the shipping office and watched, for an indifferent moment or two, the swift cortège of a late funeral racing up the hill. It flashed along the water front like a train of cellulose beetles, black and glittering, each of the thirty cars a reflection of the glare of sun on sea. He wondered, as the cars leaped away up the avenue of jade and carmine villas, eyeless in the bright evening under closed white shades, why funerals in Salandar were always such races, unpompous and frenzied, as if they were really chasing the dead. He wondered too why he never saw them coming back again. They dashed in black undignified weeping haste to somewhere along the sea-coast, where blue and yellow fishing boats beat with high moonlike prows under rocks ashen with burned seaweed, and then vanished forever.

He let the blind fall into place again, leaning spare brown elbows on the mahogany lid of his desk. He was thinking that that evening a ship would be in. It could not matter which ship — he was pretty sure it was the *Alacantara* — since nobody in his senses ever came to Salandar in the summer. There would in any case be no English passengers and he would meet it out of pure routine. After that he would go home to his small hotel and eat flabby oil-soaked *espada* that had as much taste in it as a bath sponge and drink export beer and read the English papers of a week last Wednesday. In the street outside men would sit on dark doorsteps and spit golden melon seeds into gutters, coughing with tubercular mournfulness. The flash of an open-air cinema down the street would drench the plum-black air above the surrounding courtyards with continuous gentle fountains of light, above little explosions of applause and laughter. In one of the old houses behind the hotel a woman would lull her baby to sleep with a prolonged soft song that was probably as old as the moon curve of the fishing boats that lined the shore. Under the infinite stars the red beacons on the radio masts would flame like big impossible planets above the mass of the fortress that obscured, with its vast and receding walls, nearly half the sky. And that would be his evening: a lonely and not surprising conclusion to a tiring day when nothing had happened, simply because nothing ever happened in summer in Salandar.

From across the quayside, out on the landing pier, he suddenly heard the sound of more voices than he thought was customary. He got up and parted the slats of the window shade. The pier was massed with emigrants, emigrant baggage, emigrant noises, the messy struggle of emigrant farewells. He remembered then that the *Alacantara* was not coming in. It was the *Santa Maria,* coming from precisely the opposite way.

That sort of trick of memory always overtook him at the height of summer, two months after the tourist season had died. It was the delayed shock of seasonal weariness. He was as unprepared for it as he was unprepared for the sight of the *Santa Maria* herself, a ship of pale green hulls with funnels of darker green, suddenly coming round the westerly red-black cliffs of the bay. It made him less annoyed to think that he had to meet her. He did not like to hurry. There was no need to hurry. There was nothing to hurry for. He was not going anywhere. He was not meeting anyone. The point of his meeting a ship on which he had no passenger was purely one of duty. Like most of the rest of his life on Salandar it was a bore.

Was there a passenger? With the precision of habit he turned up a black ledger of passengers' names that gave him nothing in answer. It was nice to be assured, anyway, that he was not mistaken.

A moment later he called to the only clerk to tell the porter that he wanted the launch in five minutes. His voice was dry from the summer catarrh that came from living low down, at sea level, in the rainless months, in the sandy dust of the port. He cleared his throat several times as he went out into the street and the sun struck him below the eyebrows with pain. On the corner of the pavement he stood and closed his eyes briefly before he crossed to the water front and as he opened them again the last black beetle of the funeral cortège flashed past him, expensively glittering, lurching dangerously, chasing the dead: a car filled with weeping men.

2

ON THE SHIP the air seemed absorbent. It sucked up the life of the fanless purser's cabin on the middle deck.

"She got on at Lisbon, Mr. Manson," the purser said. "She said she cabled you from there."

A small quantity of pearl-gray luggage, splashed with varnished scarlet labels, among them the letter V, stood by the purser's door. Staring down at it, Manson tried to remember back through a long drowsy day to some point where a cable might have blown in, rushed past him and, like the cortège of racing mourners, disappeared. He could not recall any cable and the purser said:

"I had better take her luggage up. I promised to look after her." He began to pick up suitcases, tucking the smallest under his arms. "She seems to like being looked after. Perhaps you will bring the last one, Mr. Manson? Thank you."

No one else had come aboard except a harbor policeman in flabby gray ducks, so thin that he seemed impossibly weighed down by black bayonet and revolver, and a customs officer in crumpled washed-out sienna gabardine. These two stood sweating at the head of the companionway, the policeman with thumbs in his drooping belt. There was not even the usual collection of hotel porters' caps on the ship, simply because every hotel was closed.

"Where is she staying?" Manson called. "There isn't a single hotel open."

"I told her that. She said she did not mind. I told her you would see all about it."

"She's nothing to do with me."

"She's English. I told her you would do it —"

"Do what? I'm not a sight-seeing guide for anybody who comes and dumps themselves down here in the middle of summer."

He felt his hands grow sweaty on the high-polished fabric of the suitcase handle. He knew, he thought, all that English women could be. Ill clad in worsted, horribly surpliced in porridge-colored shantung, they arrived some-

times as if expecting the island to yield the horse-drawn
charm of 1890, where everything could be had or done
by the clapping of hands.

"Anyway I had no warning," he said. "What warning
had I?"

He thought he saw the customs officer grin at this, and
it annoyed him further.

"She said she cabled you herself, Mr. Manson," the
purser said.

"I've seen no sign of a cable," he said. "And anyway
cable or no cable —"

"It was awfully good of you to meet me," a voice said.

When he turned, abruptly, at the same time as the
sweat-bright faces of the policeman, the customs officer
and the purser, he saw her standing behind him: a tall
black-haired girl, with an amazing combination of large
pure blue eyes and black lashes, her hair striped across the
front with a leonine streak of tawny blond.

He found himself at once resenting and resisting this
paler streak of hair.

"It was really very good of you," she said. "My name
is Vane."

He checked an impulse to say "Spelt in which way?"
and she held out a hand covered with a long cream glove.
This glove, reaching to her elbow, matched a sleeveless
dress of light cool linen.

"I know you think I've come at the wrong time of year," she said.

"Not at all."

"No?" she said. "I thought I heard you say so."

He was so irritated that he was not really conscious of helping her down the gangway. He felt instead that the gangway had begun to float on air. It was nothing but a shaky ladder of cotton reels swaying above the calm sea. It seemed almost perpendicular, pitching him forward as he went down first and waited to help her into the launch below.

The red triangular pennant of the company drooped above the burnished deckhouse and she said, staring beyond it:

"Everyone told me it was so brilliant. So much flashing color. But the rocks are black. It looks burnt out, somehow."

"That's just the summer," he said.

Out of politeness he stared with her at the shore. He thought there was a great deal of color. It was simply that it was split into a fractional mosaic of blacks and browns, of bleached pinks and the dull ruby reds of housetops half smothered by green. A tower of pale yellow, the new school, was raised like a fresh sugar stick above the black sand of the shore, at the end of which an astonishing summer residence of blue tiles, polished as a kitchen stove, was wedged into the cliff. Two or three rowing boats, piled with white baskets, with curtains of island embroideries in scarlet and green, were motionless on the oily bay, where in the high season a hundred of them clamored about liners like fighting junks, manned by brown shivering men diving for coins. Lines of high-prowed fishing boats, upcurved like horns, striped in green and blue and ocher, were pulled up along the water front, and far away and high above them he could see the water splash of a spouting *levada,* poised like gathered spittle in a fissure of rock and eucalyptus forest, pure white in blinding sun.

He suddenly felt himself defending all he saw. He wanted to say that there was plenty of color. Only the sun, burning ferociously, created an illusion of some-thing cindery, melting dully away.

"It's just a question of —"

"Oh! My bag," she said.

She stood on the lowest rung of the gangway, lifting helpless arms, imploring him with a smile.

"In my cabin — so sorry — twenty-three — you'll see it. Probably on the bed."

As he mounted the ladder quickly, more insecure than when he had come down, he remembered that cabin twenty-three was one of four on the boat deck and he walked straight for it, before the purser could speak or stop him.

He found her handbag on the bed. Unstripped, the bed was disorderly and the bag, which was why she had forgotten it, was partly covered by her pillow. Its clasp sprang open as he picked it up. Its white jaws spilled lipstick and handkerchief, a few letters, a mirror, a little diary in black morocco.

He felt intensely curious and wanted to open the diary. The bag gave out a perfume that floated about him for a moment, arousing in him a startling sensation of intimacy.

Then he felt nervous and shut the bag quickly and rushed out of the cabin, only to find the purser coming to meet him on the deck, saying:

"What was it, Mr. Manson? Was it something you could not find?"

He went on without answering, slipping hastily once again on the insecure mahogany cotton reels of the gangway, down to a sea where the launch's scarlet pennant and the yellow dress were the only things that did not melt and sway.

"You were very quick," she said. "It was very kind of you."

The sea was so calm that it was possible for himself and the girl to stand motionless on the launch all the way from the ship to shore. She stood erectly looking about her, searching the bay, the shore and the abrupt hills above the town for color.

"It surprises me," she said. "I'd expected something more exotic."

"It's exotic in winter," he said. "It's all color then. You should have come in the winter. That's when everybody comes."

It suddenly struck him that, after all, she was really not looking at the approaching shore. Something about her eyes made them seem glazed with preoccupation.

"I'm afraid it was my fault about the cable," she said. "It should have been sent. But I was in a dreadful hurry. I made up my mind all of a sudden and then somehow —"

"I don't know what you had in mind about hotels."

"I suppose they're all shut," she said.

"All the recognized ones."

"Where do you live? In one not recognized?"

"I wouldn't recommend it," he said.

Forgetfulness about the cable, forgetfulness about the bag — he stood pondering uncertainly, staring at the approaching harbor pier, wondering where to take her.

"I do apologize about the cable," she said. "I'm afraid you're peeved."

"I was trying to think of a possible solution to the hotel problem."

"It's no problem," she said. "I'm not particular. I shall find something. I always do."

"Had you any idea of how long you were staying?"

"As long as I like it."

"It isn't always possible to leave when you think you will," he said. "Ships are very irregular here. They don't just happen when you think they're going to."

"Does anything?" she said.

The launch began to make its curve to the landing pier, the change of course uplifting the scarlet pennant very slightly. Above steps of baked white concrete a line of idle taxis stretched out, with a few ox carts, in the shade of flowerless jacarandas. A smell of oil and hot bullock dung and rotting seaweed seethed in the air and he said:

"I'm afraid you'll find anything down here in the port very hot."

As the launch came into the jetty he leaped out. On the steps he held out his hand to her and she lifted the long cream glove.

"The man will bring the bags up to the top," he said.

At the top of the jetty he realized with concern that she was hatless. Heat struck down on concrete and then back again as if pitilessly forced down through a tube, dangerously compressed under the high enclosure of hills.

"I hope you're all right?" he said. "I mean the heat? The air is terribly clear and you don't always realize —"

"I don't feel it," she said. "I never feel it." She touched her hair, running her fingers through it. The paler streak of it, uplifted, exposed the mass of pure black hair below, and he realized how thick and strong and wiry it was. Its heavy sweep, shot with the curious blond streak, aroused in him the same odd sensation of uneasy intimacy he had experienced in the cabin, smelling the perfume of the handbag, by the disordered bed.

For a moment longer she stood engrossed by the sight of him staring at her hair, and he did not realize how absorbed and uncomfortable it had made him feel until she said:

"Where do we go from here? Where can I get a taxi?"

"I was thinking you could come to the office and leave your things —"

"I'd rather get a hotel," she said. "What's the name of yours?"

"Mafalda," he said. "It's terribly small and they don't really cater —"

"It doesn't matter if it's reasonable and the beds are clean. Are the beds clean?"

"Quite clean."

She looked at him without any kind of disturbance, the clear, rather too large blue eyes fixing him with exacting softness, and said:

"I think any beds that are clean enough for you ought to be clean enough for me."

"You can always try it temporarily."

From the hot taxi she leaned her long body forward and looked at the mounting hillside. Above it successive folds of rock, exposed in crags that seemed sun-blackened,

submerged under encrustations of blue-green forests of
pine and eucalyptus, fascinated her large blue eyes into
a larger stare.

"What's up there?" she said. "I mean the other side of
the mountain?"

"Not much," he said. "More rock and forest and so on.
Not many people. Over the other side there's a power station. It's lonely. There are places you can't get to."

She smiled and sat back beside him on the seat, wrap-
ping the surprisingly cool cream gloves deftly one over
the other.

"That's where I'd like to go," she said.

Then, without attaching importance to what she said,
without really giving it another thought, he was inspired
to remark with sudden cheerfulness that there would
probably be, at the hotel, a cup of tea.

3

THERE WERE MICE in the upper ceilings of the old hotel
and he lay listening to them half the night, turning over
in his mind what seemed to him the vexing problem of her
being there, in that highly unsuitable, dark, cheap hotel
where no English visitor ever came except for a temporary
night, in sheer high-season desperation. He had carefully
warned her a number of times that the food would not be

English. "It will be oily and all that," he said. "It's something it takes a long time to get used to." When she reminded him that he at any rate appeared to survive it he did not dare tell her that it was simply because he could not afford anything else. He had just had to get used to it; and now he did not ask for anything better and in his limited way he was perfectly happy. At least he supposed he was.

But something troubled him much more than this. He was perplexed and worried by a phrase she had used.

"What are you going to do with yourself?" he asked her. "It can be terribly exhausting at this time of the year —"

"I'm going to poke about," she said. "I want things to do. I want to see things."

He grew increasingly uneasy about this as the evening went on. It was not a good thing to poke your nose into things in Salandar. It was a place, in the right season, in the delicious winter flowery days, of infinite surface charm. Bougainvillaeas covered with steep massive curtains of purple and sienna-rose all the dry ravines coming down from the hills; starry scarlet poinsettias lined the potato patches; a honey odor of incense trees hung over the old streets at nighttime. If underneath all this there were people who had not enough to eat, who were afraid of something or somebody, who were tubercular or illiterate or superfluous or resentful, that was no concern of visitors.

"Don't you ever poke about and find out how things really are?" she said.

"No."

"Have you been here long?" she said. "How many years have you been here?"

"I came here about three and a half years ago. Nearly four."

It was getting so long ago he could hardly remember exactly. His time there had gradually become, in the Salandar fashion, a succession of dull tomorrows.

"How long is it since you went over to the other side of the island?" she said.

"I'm afraid I've never been over to the other side."

"By the way you spoke I thought you'd been there often," she said.

"No," he said, "I've never been there."

"Haven't you any inclination at all to see what it's like?"

"Not particularly."

It seemed to him that she did not speak her questions so much as impose them on him with the too large, too brilliant, uneasy eyes.

"What about Santo Carlo?" she said. "They say that's very interesting. Have you been there?"

No: he had not been to Santo Carlo either.

He found, presently, what seemed to him a happy solution to her restlessness, to the problem of what she should do with herself. It was also a tremendous relief to be able at last to change an uncomfortable subject.

"You could join the club," he said. "I don't know why I didn't think of it before."

"Do you belong?"

"Not now," he said. "I gave it up."

In winter the club was crowded with visitors he did not know; in summer there was no one there. After six months of it he had not considered it worth while to renew the subscription. He decided he would save the money. He had to think of the future.

"What happens there?"

"People play bridge and tennis and that sort of thing and there's a small golf course," he said. "It's rather beautiful," and then added, as if it was an extra thought to impress her: "You can get tea."

She did not say anything and he went on:

"You can get a temporary subscription — I think for even a week. I can find out for you — but then if you don't know how long you're going to stay —"

"That was something I was going to talk to you about," she said.

In speaking of the times of ships he felt more certain of himself. That at least was his job.

"It depends where you want to go from here," he said. "If you'll give me some idea of times and places I'll have —"

"When is the next ship in?"

"There'll be nothing in this week. Not until after the week end," he said. "Then the *Alacantara* is due. She's pleasant."

"It would be nice just to have the sailing times of what's likely to be coming in," she said. "Could you? It would be very sweet of you."

She had asked him so many questions that this final acutely personal one, delivered more softly, in a lowered voice, made him more uneasy than he had been before. He did not grasp even that the conversation had been largely about himself. He felt only another rush of feeling about her: a repetition of the sensation he had had in the cabin, over the handbag and the disorderly bed, and from the way she had run her fingers through her thick black hair.

"You look tired," she said to him at last. "It's time you got into that good clean bed."

In the morning he woke to an air that had in it the breath of ashes. It sprang at his already catarrhal throat with windy choking heat. He grasped then the reason for his lethargy of the previous day, his soporific irritations as he met the boat that he had not expected. The *leste* was blowing: the wind from the northeast that burned with pure incineration off the mainland sand.

This had not prevented Miss Vane from getting up at five o'clock and watching the night boats, like slowly extinguishing fireflies, bringing in their fish across the bay.

"They looked wonderful," she said. "Haven't you ever seen them come in?"

"No."

"I talked to some of them — the men, I mean. There were two brothers from Santo Carlo —"

"You should be very careful how you talk to these people," he said.

At breakfast, which they had together in the already shuttered little dining room, in a queer kind of morning twilight through which even her large and exceptionally blue eyes looked almost white in their diffusion, he warned her about the intolerable burning wind.

"It will probably last for two days," he said. "Perhaps three. I'm afraid you'll find it very exhausting."

In a white dress of low cut, with a transparent organdie insertion across the breast, she looked remarkably cool and she said:

"Isn't it a good chance to get up into the hills? Couldn't you take a day off and come with me?"

He rested easily on the firm ground of his local knowledge.

"That's the curious thing about the *leste*," he said. "It's even hotter in the hills. You'd hardly believe it, but the coast is going to be the cooler place."

"I might go myself."

"Oh, no!" he said. "Don't think of doing that."

"Why not?"

"Oh! In the first place — Well, it's hardly the thing. You see you can only drive so far. After that it's a question of mule track. You need several days —"

"I have plenty of days."

"Yes, but not while the *leste* is on," he said. "Really not. It can be absolutely ghastly up there when the *leste* is on."

"How would you know?" she said. "You've never been."

His coffee, which should have been cool after so much conversation, sprang down his already anguished throat like hot acid. He felt unable to speak for some moments and at last she said:

"I think you look awfully tired. Don't you ever want to get away from here?"

"Not particularly. I suppose eventually —"

"Not when the ships come in? Don't you ever suddenly feel, hell, for God's sake let me get away — don't you ever feel like that?"

"I can't say I do."

"I think it might do you good to get away."

For a second he was touched, and then bewildered, by her concern. He was disturbed too because she had, as he now noticed for the first time, no coffee to drink.

"Didn't you have any coffee?"

"I had orange instead," she said. "It's cooler."

"I suppose I ought to have done that," he said. "But I

always have coffee. I can't get out of the habit of it somehow —"

"Would you come on this trip to the hills?" she said.
"I honestly don't know."

"I shall go," she said. "I'll fix it up. I like fixing things.
Would you come if I fixed it?"

"It's awfully difficult for me to say," he said. "You see,
everybody's on leave. Charlton, my chief, is on leave. The
only really good local clerk has gone to Lisbon for a week.
It's very doubtful if I could leave the office in any case —"

"You've got the week end."

"I know, but —" He found himself being helplessly
absorbed, as his breath had been absorbed in the stifling
purser's cabin on the ship, by her enlarged diffused eyes,
almost pure white, their true color extinguished until they
gave out a curious impression of nakedness in the dark
morning shadow. "And apart from anything else there's
the *leste* —"

"If we wait till the *leste* is over?" she said. "If it blows
for two or three days it ought to be over by the week end,
oughtn't it?"

"Well, you can't tell —"

"Shall we chance it?" she said. "Shall I fix it up?"

"Will it do if I decide this evening?"

"I'm going to fix it during the day," she said. "If the
Alacantara comes next week I haven't much time."

"All right," he said. "I suppose I could come."

As she got up from the table she smiled and touched his arm, telling him to drink his coffee. Her body was held forward to him, the partially transparent inset of her dress exposing her breast. He was aware of the falling discolored band of yellow in her intense black hair and it disturbed him again more than anything she had done or said, and as he stared at it she smiled.

"Do I look so awful?" she said. "I haven't combed my hair since I went down to the harbor. I must go and do it now."

He called after her to ask what she was going to do with herself all day. "You must take it easily. Don't go and exhaust yourself," he said.

"I'll probably swim," she called back from the stairs.

"Be careful of the swell," he said. "It's terribly deceptive. It can sometimes be twenty or thirty feet even on the calmest days." After all he had a certain responsibility for her now. "Don't go out too far."

4

THE ROAD to the central ridge of mountains wound up through gorges of gray volcanic rock, under steep declivities of pine and eucalyptus closely planted as saplings against the erosion of a sparse burned soil, red and cindrous, veined yellow here and there by courses of long-dried water. The car crept upward very slowly, beetlewise, on black setts of blistered rock that gave way, beyond the last windowless white houses, to a track of potholes sunk in gray and crimson sand.

"It was a stroke of genius to bring the cook," she said.

He did not feel that this was flattery. It really was, he thought, rather a stroke of genius on his part to think of the cook. The idea of the cook sprang from his recollection that, at the top of the mule pass, there was also a resthouse. For practically nothing you could put up there, cook meals and so on and do the thing in comfort. He was very pleased about that. It saved a lot of trouble. He didn't think he could have come all the way up that hot dreary track otherwise.

The *leste,* after all, had died. The air in the mountains was still hot, but height began to give it, as the car climbed slowly, a thinness that was fresh and crystalline. Objects began to appear so vivid that they stuck out, projected by strong blue lines that were pulsations rather than shadow. In a curious way everything was enlarged by scintillation.

Perhaps it was this that made Manson, sitting at the back of the car with Miss Vane, fix his eyes hypnotically on the black hair of the cook, sitting in front with the driver.

The head of the cook was like an ebony bowl, polished to a sheen of greasy magnificence by brushings of olive

oil. Below it the shoulders were flat and square, the erectness of them giving power to the body that was otherwise
quite short and stiff, except when it bent in sudden bows
of politeness to Miss Vane.

Sometimes the car jolted violently in and out of potholes and Manson and Miss Vane were pitched helplessly
upward and against each other, taken unawares. But the
shoulders of Manuel, the cook, were never disturbed by
more than a quiver and sometimes it seemed to Manson
that they gave a shrug.

This hypnosis about the neck of the cook lasted until
the car road ended and the mule track began, winding
away into a thick scrub of wild bay trees and stunted,
blue-needled pines. At the foot of the track the mules
were waiting, four flickering skeletons brought up by two
barefoot peasants wearing trousers of striped blue shirt
material and black trilby hats.

Manuel loaded two osier baskets of provisions, Manson's rucksack and one of Miss Vane's scarlet-labeled too-
neat suitcases onto one of the mules, and the peasants began to lead the mules up the hill.

After Manuel had shouted after them the two peasants
came back. They both looked downtrodden in protestation
and Manuel, standing over them, square and erect, looked
more assertive than before.

"What is it, Manuel?" Miss Vane said. "Is something
the matter?"

"No, madame." He pronounced his English fully and correctly, elongating the final syllable.

"What is it then?"

"They want to go with us, madame."

"That was the idea, wasn't it?" Manson said.

"It's not necessary, sir. I can manage without them."

"You know the way?" she said.

"Yes, madame," he said. "I've done it before."

After that the taxi driver drove away and the peasants disappeared up the hill. Manuel took the first and second mules, Miss Vane the third and Manson the fourth. Manson had never been on a mule before and his legs seemed so much too long that he felt gawkily ridiculous. But looking ahead, beyond Miss Vane and the provision mule to the leading figure of Manuel, he was relieved to see that Manuel looked, as he thought, still more stupid.

His preoccupation with the back of Manuel's neck had been so absorbed that he had not really noticed that Manuel was wearing the black suit of a waiter. And as Manuel turned to look back at the column Manson saw that he was wearing the tie, the shirt front and the collar too.

It took three hours to climb through paths among bay tree and pine and tree heath and an occasional eucalyptus stunted by height to the size of a currant bush, as far as the resthouse. As the mules marched slowly upward, jerky and rhythmical, the mountains seemed to march rapidly forward, shutting in the heat and shutting out much of the sky. And as the heat developed oppressively Manson called once to Miss Vane:

"You'd hardly think there would be snow up here, would you?"

"There is no snow up here, sir."

"I thought there was always snow. After all, it's six thousand —"

"Not on this side, sir. You're thinking of the Santo Carlo side. There is never snow just here."

Manson did not speak again and it was half an hour before he noticed, glinting in the sun, what he thought were iron sheds of the power station framed in a gap ahead.

"I rather think that's the new power station," he called to Miss Vane. "They had great difficulty in getting the pipes up there —"

"That's not the power station, sir. That's the old pumping station for the *levadas*. They don't use it now."

"Where is the power station?" Miss Vane said.

"It's over the other side, madame. You won't be able to see it from this direction."

"And where is the place you can see the two coasts from?" she said. "You know — the sea both sides?"

"You will be able to go there from the resthouse,

madame," he said. "It isn't far. You'll be able to climb up there."

Manson stretched out his hand and snatched at a leaf of a eucalyptus tree, crushing it sharply with his fingers and then lifting the leaf to his nose. The harsh oily odor of eucalyptus was unpleasant and irritated him. It reminded him of times when, as a child, his chest had been very bad and he had coughed a lot and he had not been able to get his breath.

He unconsciously kept the leaf in his hand until, at the suggestion of Manuel, they stopped to rest. "We are half-way now, madame," Manuel said.

Manuel poured glasses of export beer for Manson and Miss Vane and served them with stiff politeness and then retired to a respectful distance among the mules. From masses of rock above them, studded with pale flat cacti that were like blown roses of delicate green, water dripped in large slow drops, like summery thundery rain.

"Well, this is marvelous," Miss Vane said and lifted her glass to him, smiling with huge blue eyes in which Manson felt he could see all the summery wateriness and the great scintillation of mountain sky.

He lifted his glass to her in return, re-experiencing a sudden rush of the intimacy he had felt over her disheveled bed and her handbag and that recurred whenever he looked at the yellow streak in her hair. He had a wild idea that presently, at the resthouse, they might be alone together.

"There's an awful smell of eucalyptus," Miss Vane said.

He flushed, pounding with anger at himself, and said: "I'm afraid it's me. I crushed a leaf. Don't you like it?"

"I loathe it," she said. "I can't bear it near me. I hate it. You'll have to go and wash your hands."

He went away in silence and washed his hands among the cacti, under a spilling cleavage of rock. The water was icy in the brilliant, burning air. He washed his hands carefully and then smelled them and it seemed that the smell of eucalyptus remained. Then he washed them again with slow, rejected, clinical care.

It was not until the resthouse came in sight that he emerged from a painful and articulate silence during which he had done nothing but stare at the sweat oozing slowly and darkly down the mule's neck. He was pleasantly startled by hearing Miss Vane call back:

"Hullo there. Asleep?" Her voice was solicitous and friendly once more and was accompanied by a sidelong dazzling smile. "You can see the resthouse. We're nearly there."

"I think it was the beer," he said. "Made me drowsy —"

"Look at it," she said. "It's exciting, isn't it? I'm excited."

"Oh, yes! It's bigger than I thought —"

"Aren't you excited?" she said. "This is really something. This is what I wanted."

The track had widened. She reined the mule and waited for him. Then as she turned the mule half-face to him he noticed the shape of her body, pressed heavily across the dark animal flanks. She had ridden up in a sleeveless thin white dress, the skirt of which was drawn up beyond her knees. He had never been able to make up his mind how old she was and now, in her excitement, her skirt drawn up above bare smooth legs, her eyes enormously shining, he thought she seemed much younger than she had done down in the scorching, withering period of the *leste,* in the town. She seemed to have left her hostile restlessness behind.

"Oh, it's marvelous and it really wasn't far, was it?" she said. "It didn't seem an hour. It was easy after all."

He said he didn't think it had been far either and he was aware suddenly that Manuel had gone ahead. The impossible waiter suit, mule-mounted, was almost at the veranda steps. A hundred yards separated him from Manson and Miss Vane, and again an overpowering sense of intimacy came over Manson, so that he felt tremulously stupid and could not speak to her.

"Now aren't you glad I made you come?" she said.

"Yes," he said.

"Back there I thought you were mad with me."

"Oh, no!"

"Not the smallest piece?"

He shook his head. "Not a little bit," he said.

The smile went temporarily out of her face. The mule jerked nervously ahead. "I really thought you were mad," she said and it did not occur to him until long afterwards that she might have hoped he had been.

5

FROM MANUEL, during the rest of that day and the succeeding day, came an almost constant sound of whistling that jarred and irritated Manson like the scrape of a file. The resthouse, neat and clean, with something not unlike a chapel about its bare whitewashed coolness, was divided into three parts. In the large central room Manson and Miss Vane ate at a long mahogany table the meals that Manuel prepared in a kitchen that ran along the north side of a large birdlike cage made of gauze. In this cage Manuel kept up the whistling that continued to infuriate Manson even at nighttime, as he tried to sleep in the third part, composed of his own bedroom and Miss Vane's on the western side.

Miss Vane was a woman who hated trousers.

"I was born a woman and I'll dress like one," she said. So she had ridden astride the mule in a loose cool white dress instead of the slacks Manson thought would have been more suitable, even though he disliked them. And all that day and most of the next, Sunday, she lay in front of the resthouse in a sun suit of vivid green that was boned so tight to the shape of her body that it was like an extra, gleaming skin.

As she lay in the sun Manson was aware of two sorts of feeling about her. When she lay on her back he saw the Miss Vane he had met on the ship; the Miss Vane of the hotel and the town, of the advancing, blistering *leste*; the Miss Vane incorrigibly and restlessly prodding him into coming to the mountains. She was the Miss Vane with the startling, discomforting tongue of yellow across her black hair. She was uneasy and he could not get near her.

When she turned over and lay on her face he could not see the yellow streak in her hair. Her head was one gentle mass of pure black, undisrupted by that one peroxide streak that always set him quivering inside. The black-haired Miss Vane did not startle him. She seemed quiet and untroubled. He wanted to thrust his face down into the plain unsullied mass of her thick black hair and let himself speak with tenderness of all sorts of things.

Always, at the point when he felt he could do this, she turned over on her back, lifting the front of her body straight and taut in the sun. The peroxide streak flared up. The eyes, too blue and too brilliant, flashed with exactly the same sort of unreality, as if she had dyed them too.

"Tomorrow we must do something," she said. "We can't lie here forever."

"It's very pleasant lying here."

"We must go up to the place where you can see the two coasts. We'll start early and go all day," she said. "By the way, I've been meaning to ask you. You must have come out here very young. How old are you?"

"Twenty-seven," he said.

"I beat you by a year," she said. "It's old, isn't it? We're creeping on. Don't you sometimes feel it's old — all of it slipping away from you? Life and that sort of thing?"

He could hear Manuel whistling in the distance, in the bird cage, and he could see the paler streak in Miss Vane's hair as she turned and stared at the sky.

"I must say I thought you were older," she said.

He was listening to the inexhaustibly dry, infuriating whistle of Manuel.

"You don't look older," she said, "but I think you act older. But then men of your age often do."

She lifted one hand to shade her eyes from the glare of sun.

"The sun gets terrific power by midday," she said. "I think I ought to have my glasses. Would you fetch them — do you mind?"

He got up and began to walk away and she called after him:

"In the bedroom. Probably with my dress. I left them there when I changed."

In the bedroom he remembered the cabin on the ship. He remembered how she liked things to be done for her. But now the bed, neatly made by Manuel, was not disheveled. It was only her clothes that lay untidily about where she had undressed and thrown them down. He could not find the sunglasses. They were not with her dress. He picked up her clothes several times and finally laid them in a chair. The glasses were not in her handbag and they were not on the bed.

His inability to find the glasses startled him into nervousness. He approached the bed with trembling hands. He pulled back the coverlet and put his hands under the pillow and let them rest there. He wanted all of a sudden to lie down on the bed. He was caught up in an illusion of lying with her there.

He went quickly out into the sun. From the ledge of short grass, walled by rock, where Miss Vane was lying, he heard voices. And as he came closer he saw that Miss Vane was wearing her sunglasses.

"It's all right — Manuel found them. I'd left them in the dining room."

Manuel, in shirt sleeves, without the black waiter's coat, stood stifly erect, holding a bunch of two or three roses in his hands.

"Don't you think that's amazing?" Miss Vane said. "He even finds roses up here."

"Where on earth do you get roses?" Manson said.

"In the garden, sir. At the back."

"He says there was a wonderful garden here once. An Englishman made it. He used to come here for the summer. He was a sugar planter or something. Wasn't that it, Manuel?"

Manuel's eyes rested thinly and dryly on some point across the valley.

"Yes, madame. He was sugar. He was sugar, wine, sugar brandy, coal, sardines, water, everything." He spoke slowly. "He took the water from the people and sold it back again."

"You mean he developed the country," Manson said.

"That's so, sir."

Manuel walked away and Manson looked after him. He detected, for the first time, an oddity in Manuel's walk. The right foot, swinging outwardly, stubbed the ground as it came back again. And this weakness, not quite a deformity, suddenly deprived the stocky shoulders of their power.

"Are you looking at his leg?" Miss Vane said. "He was in an accident or something. With his brother. He was telling me before breakfast. Before you came down. Did he tell you?"

"No."

"I feel rather sorry for him," she said.

He sat down in the sun, his mind searching for a change of subject. He stared across the valley, remembering with what thin, dry abstraction Manuel had looked there.

"Oh! I just remembered," he said. "After the *Alacantara* on Wednesday there isn't another decent boat for three weeks."

"No wonder you get a feeling of isolation here."

"Well, anyway I thought you ought to know. It's a long time."

"Would you find it long?"

He wanted to say "It depends." He wanted to qualify, somehow, the statement he had already made. He knew that what he had to say and feel depended on Miss Vane and whether Miss Vane caught the *Alacantara*. Already he did not want her to catch it. He was afraid of her catching it. But he could not express what he felt and he said:

"That damned man is always whistling. Can you hear it? He's always whistling."

"I hadn't noticed it."

When they went in to lunch Manuel stood behind her chair, holding it, pushing it gently forward as she sat down.

As he prepared to serve soup she suddenly waved her hands with impatience at herself and said:

"My bag. Would you think I could be such a dim-wit? I leave it everywhere —"

"I will get it, madame," Manuel said.

He hurried out of the room with dignified jerky steps.

"I could have got it for you," Manson said.

"I know you could." The large flashing blue eyes disarmed him. "But he likes doing things. He would be hurt if we didn't let him. That's what he's here for."

Manuel came and put Miss Vane's bag on the table.

"Thank you, Manuel," she said.

Manuel served soup from a wicker trolley.

"By the way," she said, "we would like to do the climb to the top. How long will it take us?"

"It isn't a climb, madame," Manuel said. "It's just a walk. It takes half an hour."

"You and your inaccessible places," she said to Manson. "Everything is too easy for words."

"What about the Serra?" Manson said. "That isn't easy, is it?"

"I do not know the Serra, sir."

"What is the Serra?" she said.

"It's the high plateau," Manson said. "The really high one. The really lonely one. Isn't that so, Manuel? It's lonely. People don't like it, do they?"

"No, sir," Manuel said. "People don't like it."

"Why not?" she said.

"I can't say, madame," he said. "I think it's because there's nothing there. People like to have company. They don't like places where there is nothing."

"I think that's where we should go," Manson said. "That would be something worth while."

"I don't think so, sir."

"Oh! I most certainly think so," Manson said. "After all, that's what we came up here for — the high places and the view and that sort of thing."

"If the view is no better," Miss Vane said, "there's hardly any point in going, is there? Is the view any better?"

"I don't think you can see so far, madame," Manuel said.

"Well, there you are," she said.

With irritation Manson said: "I thought you were the adventurous one. I thought you liked it the difficult way."

"Oh! I do," she said. "But if there's no point — I mean if Manuel doesn't think the thing worth while —"

Manson waited for Manuel to clear the soup dishes and take them away through the gauze doors that separated the dining room from his cage at the back.

"I fail to see what Manuel has to do with it," he said. "We can go alone. Manuel isn't obliged to come."

"What is there about this place?" she said.

"He's afraid of it. They're all afraid of it. They're superstitious about it."

"Is there anything to be superstitious about?"

"Not a thing."

"Then why do you suppose they're superstitious?"

"They hate being alone," he said.

"Don't you?" she said.

"Not a bit," he said. "I rather like it —" Abruptly he realized what he had said and he felt his confidence, which had been mounting and strengthening, suddenly recede. Confusedly he tried to retrieve it and said:

"I didn't mean it quite like that — I meant I liked being alone in the sense that I wasn't frightened of it —"

"Oh! It doesn't matter," she said. "Here comes the food. It looks like sort of pie — is it, Manuel? Is it pie?"

"Yes, madame," he said. "It is steak and kidney pie. Made in the English way."

After lunch, as they had coffee outside, under a tree he kept telling her was an arbutus, though he was not sure and it was only a way of getting his confidence back, she said:

"About this place. Would you like to go?"

"I'd like to," he said.

Her eyes, always so large and incorrigibly assertive and apparently forceful, seemed suddenly uncertain. She ran her hand across the streak of paler hair and said:

"It isn't one of those evil places, is it? You know — nothing to do with the dead?"

"It's just high and lonely," he said. "It's the crowning point of the island. That's all."

She stared across the valley, to a far glitter of sun on harsh iron rock, and Manson remembered how Manuel had stared across the valley too.

"You'd really like to go, wouldn't you?" she said. "We'd have to go alone, I suppose? Manuel wouldn't come."

He felt an ascendant rush of triumph at the thought of being alone with her.

"I don't think it need bother us," he said. "It isn't that far."

For a moment she did not answer. She had slipped off the dress she had put on to cover her sun suit during lunch and once again he found himself thinking how taut and mature her body looked, emerging naked and smooth pale brown from the costume of vivid green. If only he could have rubbed out, somehow, the disturbing streak of paler hair.

"You really think it's not one of those evil places?" she said. "Nothing to do with the dead?"

"No more than anywhere else has."

"Only I couldn't bear it," she said, "if it had anything to do with the dead. And it's been so easy so far."

6

THEY ARRANGED to start next morning at nine; but when Manson came out of his bedroom and went out onto the veranda he discovered Miss Vane and Manuel talking at the foot of the steps. Manuel had rigged up a pole on which, at each end, he had hooked a basket for luncheon. As he saw Manson coming he hoisted the pole to his shoulder, balancing the basket on the curved smooth pole.

With vexation Manson said: "I thought Manuel wasn't coming."

"He's coming as far as lunch," Miss Vane said. "Then if we want to go on any farther —"

"Of course we want to go farther, don't we?" he said. "We want to do the whole thing."

"He says that's up to us."

"It's amazing how people fold up when it comes to it," Manson said. "Good God, you might think it was Everest or something."

"Well, it's probably as well he is coming," she said. "We'd only have to carry the lunch baskets and it's going to be awfully hot."

Manuel, who had not spoken, began to walk on ahead. Miss Vane followed him and Manson walked some paces behind her. The sunlight behind him was already so crystalline in its subalpine transparence that it shone in Miss

Vane's hair with a remarkable effect of edging it with minute thorns of tawny gold.

Presently, across the steep short valley, he could see the high edge of the central plateau. It surprised him, in that first moment, by having something domestic about it. It emerged as a vast and domestic piece of pumice stone abandoned between two vaster shoulders of naked rock. In the strong sunlight he could have sworn that these rocks, perpendicular and iron gray and treeless to the foot, shot off a spark or two that flashed like signals across the lower valley.

"That's where we're going," he said to Miss Vane. "See? Up there."

"It looks farther off than I thought," she said.

"We've got all day," he said. "After all it's only Monday — you don't have to catch the *Alacantara* today."

As he spoke of the *Alacantara* he remembered the town: Monday morning, the drawn sun-shutters of the office, the spiritless flat dustiness of rooms shut up for the week end, the horrible Monday lassitude. A signal from the opposing rocks across the valley shot off with a trick of winking semaphore and expressed his astonished joy at being no longer part of that awful office, watching the cabs on the water front, the listless bootblacks rocking on the pavements, the funerals racing away up the hill.

He realized, with a remarkable surge of confidence, that he was free.

"By the way, are you going to catch the *Alacantara*? Have you made up your mind?"

"Not quite."

"I know her captain," he said. "I'd come aboard with you and see that he knew who you were."

She turned and held out her hand suddenly and said:

"There's room for you to walk on the track with me. Come on. I hate walking alone."

A fragment of his hesitation came back.

"Come on," she said. "Come and walk with me. I hate the feeling of someone being just behind me."

She reached out and caught his hand and they walked abreast.

"That's better," she said. "Now I feel you're with me."

Sometimes the swaying coolielike scales of Manuel's baskets disappeared beyond dark shoulders of rock. Manson felt then that Manuel was not part of himself and Miss Vane. He looked up at the enlarging plateau, assuring himself of its unexciting domesticity, feeling contemptuous of people like Manuel who saw it as a formidable and fearsome thing.

At the same time the feeling grew on him also that Miss Vane was slightly afraid. That was why she wanted him to walk with her; that was why she would ask him now and then if he still wanted to go to the top. He had the increasing impression too that she had something on her mind. Perhaps that was why she was continually so forgetful of things like her handbag.

Halfway through the morning one of his shoelaces came undone. He had not brought with him very suitable shoes for walking and the best he could find that day was a pair of old canvas sandals, with rubber soles.

As he stooped to tie the shoelace Miss Vane stopped to wait for him. He had some difficulty with the shoelace and was afraid of breaking it. When he looked up again Manuel had disappeared and Miss Vane was alone, staring at something far down a long spoon-shaped gorge of rock.

His feelings at seeing her there alone gave him a sort of buoyancy. His shoes were soft on the path. He had nothing to do but creep up to her and put his hands on her hair and turn her face to him and kiss her.

Before he could do anything she turned and pointed down the gorge and said:

"There's something down there. Do you see? Right down. A house or something — two or three houses."

"Yes. They're houses," he said.

"I didn't think there were villages up here."

"It's a longish way away," he said. "Probably two or three hours by path."

"We must ask Manuel about it," she said.

His feeling of buoyancy died and when they walked on again he automatically fell into the way of walking behind her until she reminded him about it and held out her hand.

Before lunch, which Manuel laid out in a small clearing of pines, in one of those places where water dripped like summery rain from fissures of cacti-studded rock, Manuel asked her stiffly:

"Would you like something to drink before you eat, madame?"

"I would," she said. "What is there?"

"There's beer, madame," he said. "And gin."

"What gin is it?" Manson said.

"The best, sir." Manuel held up the bottle for Manson to see and Manson said:

"Good. We don't want local muck. We'll have gin."

He drank the gin rather quickly. Then, looking down over the sliced-out gorges, streamless far below, he used exactly the words Miss Vane had used on the journey up with the mules.

"Well, this is marvelous," he said. The village of obscure white houses seemed of paltry insignificance, far away. "It's absolutely marvelous, I think. Don't you?"

"It's lovely."

"I think it's stunning. How far to the top, Manuel?"

"This is as far as the track goes, sir."

"I don't get that," Manson said. "You can see a path going up there as plain as daylight. I've been watching it. You can see it going most of the way."

"It's probably made by goats, sir."

The remark seemed to Manson to have in it the slightest touch of oblique insolence, and he asked abruptly for another gin. He was very glad that Miss Vane decided to have one too.

But the lunch was good. He awarded absolutely top marks to Manuel for the lunch. A slight breeze blew off the upper mountain and cooled the glare of sun. He took another gin and was aware of the semaphore spark of signals ignited over the black of distant rocks and he remarked several times, munching on big open sandwiches of red beef and peeled eggs and ham, that food always tasted so much better in the open air.

"What is the village, Manuel?" Miss Vane said.

"That's the village of Santa Anna, madame."

"How far away is it?"

Manson said: "Several hours. It would probably take more than half a day to get there. Sometimes there are bad mists too. Then it takes more than a day."

With another gin, in which he was glad Miss Vane joined him, Manson felt all the flare of antagonism against Manuel come back. The man was a damn know-all. Too smooth by half. Too smooth. Too knowing. Worst of all too damned right.

"Good God, look — there's an eagle," he said.

A large bird, suspended between the two shoulders of

mountain, seemed to hold for a moment the entire sky in its claws.

"That's a buzzard, sir," Manuel said. "There are no eagles here."

Manson stared at the bird that seemed, with motionless deceit, to hold the sky in its claws.

"I'd like another gin," he said. "Would you?"

"I will if you will," she said.

"Good," he said. "That'll get us steamed up for the top."

7

DURING LUNCH Miss Vane took off her shoes and for some moments after lunch, when she appeared to have some difficulty in getting them on again, Manson felt impatient and disappointed.

"Oh, it's nothing. It's only that my feet ache a bit." He saw her look up at the plateau of rock that spanned and blocked, exactly like the barrier of a dam, the entire western reach of valley.

"It looks awfully far," she said.

"Don't you want to go?"

"It isn't that. I was only wondering about time."

"I thought you were the one with plenty of time," he

said. "We ought to have brought the hammock. Then we could have carried you."

He said the words rather breezily, with a smile.

"You think we can make it?" she said. "I mean in the time? Perhaps we ought to ask Manuel?"

"Oh! Damn Manuel," he said.

Manuel was washing the lunch things under a small fissure of water that broke from perpendicular rock above the path.

"Manuel — how far is it to the top?" she said. "How long should it take us?"

"You should give two hours, madame."

"There and back — or just there?"

"There and back," he said.

"Oh! That's nothing," Manson said. "That's no time."

The sight of Manuel deferentially wiping a plate with a tea cloth, in his shirt sleeves, so like a waiter who had lost his way, made him feel suddenly superior again.

"You're coming, Manuel, aren't you?" she said.

"No, madame, I'm not coming. I shall wait here for you."

A moment of strained silence seemed to be pinned, suspended, ready to drop, in the immense space of hot noon sky. With irritation Manson heard her break it by saying:

"We've got all afternoon. Won't you change your mind?"

"No thank you, madame."

"Oh, if the fellow doesn't want to come he doesn't want to come. That's that."

"I was simply asking," she said.

A moment later, fired by something between annoyance and exhilaration, he was ready to start.

"If you get tired of waiting," he said to Manuel, "you can start back. We know the way."

The path made a series of regular spiral ascents with growing sharpness, narrowing to a single-line track on which Manson and Miss Vane could well walk together. Disturbed by their feet a rock fell, flattish, skimming like a slate from a house roof, pitching down, crashing with gunshot echoes into a caldron of steamy, sunlit haze.

"It's hot, isn't it?" she said. "You don't really want to go to the top, do you?"

"Of course I do. That's what we came for, didn't we?"

She did not answer and he said:

"I don't wonder the English perfected mountaineering. None of these other chaps seem to have the slightest guts for it."

The buzzard reappeared in the sky like a growing speck of dust on glass, but this time below and not above him. He stood for a moment in intent exhilaration, watching the descending bird that was really a hundred feet or so below him now. He was amused to think that he had climbed higher than a bird in the sky, higher than Man-

uel, higher perhaps than anything but a goat or a goat-
herd had ever climbed on the island before.

"You know what?" he began to say

Another rock fell noisily. Its skimming, sliding fall,
in clean curvature into hazy space, had the breathless
beauty of a ball well thrown. He heard its crash on other
rocks below. He listened for some time to its long double-
repeated echoes across the valley. Then he realized suddenly that to his half-finished remark there had been no
answer.

He turned and saw Miss Vane already forty or fifty
feet above him. She was walking steadily. Before he could
call she turned and stared back, eyeless in her black sunglasses, and waved her hand.

"I thought you were the big mountaineer."

"Oh! Wait, wait," he said. "We must keep together."

She seemed to laugh at him before going on. He scram-
bled after her. And although she was not really hurrying
it was several minutes before he reached her. By that
time he was glad she was sitting down.

"My God, it's getting hot," he said.

"You were the one who wanted to do this."

"I know. I'm all right. We mustn't rush it, that's all.
It's like everything else — easy if you keep to a system."

"My system is to lie down at frequent intervals and
stop there," she said.

As she lay down on the ledge of short dry grass she

took off her sunglasses. The glare of sun, too harsh for her, made her suddenly turn and lie on her face, spreading out her arms. Instantly the sunlight, as it had done earlier in the day, shone on the back of her hair with the brilliant effect of edging it with minute thorns of tawny gold.

Suddenly the sensation of uneasy intimacy he had first experienced in the cabin, on the ship, above the disheveled bed, came rushing back. It became one with the intoxicating experience of having climbed higher than the buzzard on the mountain.

He turned her face and began kissing her. He remembered thinking that that was something he had not bargained for in any system — would not have bargained for it if he had planned it for a thousand years. She moved her lips in a series of small fluttering pulsations that might have been protest or acceptances — he could not tell. The impression was that she was about to let him go and then that she could not bear to let him go. The effect was to rock him gently, in warm blindness, on the edge of the gorge.

He was still in a world of spinning blood and sunlight and tilting rock when he sat up again. Her eyes were intensely blue under lowered lids in the sun. In a flash she shut them against the glare, parting her mouth at the same time.

"That was easy," she said.

"Easy?"

"I mean I didn't expect you to do it like that," she said. "I mean I thought it would be different with you."

He heard the snapped cry of a bird, like the flap of linen, the only sound in a vast and burning chasm of silence, somewhere above the extreme edge of stunted heath and pine.

"Again," she said. "It made me feel better."

Long before the end of that second kiss he was perfectly sure that she belonged to him. He was so sure that he found himself thinking of the resthouse, the dark cover of evening, the way they would be together long after the infuriating whistling Manuel had died behind the cage. He felt his pride in his confidence leap up through his body in thrusting, stabbing bursts.

"That made me feel better still," she said.

"Better?"

"Happier — that's what I mean."

Suddenly, clearly, and for the first time he found himself wondering why she had bothered to come there at the height of summer.

"Happier? Weren't you happy before?"

"We ought to have found some shadier spot," she said. "I'm melting. Can you see my bag? Where's my bag?"

He did not bother to look for the bag.

"Were you?"

"No: I wasn't," she said.

"Was that why you came here?"

"Partly."

Her eyes were shut again. In contrast he felt he saw the shape of her breasts, painfully clear under the thin white dress, stir, wake and look wonderfully up at him.

"Only partly?"

"You remember the day I came and I said there wasn't any color?"

He remembered that. It seemed a thousand years away.

"It was color I was looking for," she said.

A bird cry, another break of silence, another suspicion of a whispered echo far away between sunburned roofs of rock were enough to make him uneasy again.

"I don't quite understand," he said. "Color?"

"Where's my bag?" she said. "Can't you see my bag?"

For God's sake, he thought, the bag. Why the bag? Why did she always forget the bag?

"No, it's not here. You can't have brought it," he said.

"Oh! Didn't I?" She sat up, groping in the sun. Her eyes were wide open; he saw them blue and wet, enormous with trouble. Ineffectually he searched for the bag too, knowing it wasn't there. He knew too what she was going to ask and while he was still groping about the grass she said:

"Would you go back and get it? Would you be a dear?"

He knew suddenly that he was a fool. He was a fool and he would go down and get the bag. He was a fool and he would climb up again. In time she would lose

the bag again and he would be a fool and find it once
more.

"Must you have it? Do you need it to kiss with?"

"Don't talk like that. I'm lost without it, that's all. You
can kiss me anyway."

As she sat upright he kissed her again. He felt her give
a great start of excitement, as if all the blood were leaping
to the front of her body. Then she broke away and said:

"The bag. Couldn't you get the bag? Would you
please?"

"You're not in some kind of trouble, are you?" he said.

"No. No trouble."

"Tell me what it is."

"I'm in no trouble — honest to God, I'm not in any
trouble."

"What then?"

"I don't know — a sort of hell," she said. "Get the bag
and I'll tell you about it. You made me feel better about
it already."

Suddenly where her body had been there was space.
Some trick of refraction, a twist in the glare of sun on
whiteness, suppressed his power of sight. Instead of her
shining body there was a naked gap on the path. As he
walked down it to fetch her bag he found he could not
see very well. He was aware of groping again, his canvas
shoes slithering on scalding dark platters of rock, waking

loose stones to curve out on flights of vicious perfection to the steaming haze below.

The infuriating whistle of Manuel brought him back to himself.

"Have you seen Miss Vane's bag?" he shouted.

"Yes, sir. Here it is, sir, with the lunch things."

Manson grasped the white bag and turned to walk back up the path.

"Aren't you going to the top, sir?"

"Mind your own business!" he said. He stopped. "Oh! Another thing. I think we'll be starting back tomorrow. You'd better get back and start packing."

"Very well, sir," Manuel said.

High above the mountainside the somber hypnotic buzzard had risen again to hold the sky in its claws. It woke in Manson a sudden hatred for the place. The sky of summer seemed to reflect, in a curious harsh and lifeless glare, the depressing slatelike glaze of the high naked edge of plateau. Below, the trees were fired and lost in smoldering ashen dust. From far away a glint of steel in minute winks shot from the mass of pines with the effect of blue glass-paper.

A moment or two later he heard once again that curious sound that was like the dry flap of shaken linen, startling in the thin air. He heard it at the moment of turning the last of the spirals in the path before reaching Miss Vane.

And as he heard it and turned his head he lost his sense
of focus again, and a rock fell.

It fell this time from under his feet. It seemed to cross,
a second later, a shadow that might have been caused by
the buzzard suddenly whipping earthwards to kill. Instead
he saw that it was another rock. It fell with bewildering
swiftness from under his too-smooth canvas shoes, taking
with it a black and slaty shower.

This shower was the entire corner of the path. As it fell
it seemed to suck him down. For a second or two he was
aware of a conscious effort to save himself. Then, clutching with ferocity at Miss Vane's white bag, he fell too.

8

His impression of coming death was sharp and instanta-
neous. It was a flame leaping up to meet him like the up-
rising ball of sun. Its inescapable extinction was like the
extinction of Miss Vane's white body on the path. It was
there one moment and then, in a final trick of refraction,
was black and void.

He half picked himself up in a shower of slate and
slate dust, at the foot of a pine no taller than a man. His
left foot was jammed by rock. His fall had ended in a
kind of football tackle, not badly aimed at the feet, the
roots, of the pine. He struggled to free his foot, and the
tree roots, under his weight, cracked under the rock and

began to come out like slow-drawn teeth, in gristly pain. He thought he was laughing. Then he knew that he was really sucking air, enormous gasps of it, gorging at it, fighting for it in pure fright with his terrified mouth and tongue.

The last of the tree roots were sucked out and the tree fell over, letting him down. His foot too was free. He laughed and shouted something. He did not know what it was but the very feeling of coherent air across his tongue gave him enormous hope. He felt suddenly as calm and poised as the buzzard above the valley.

He climbed slowly up on his hands and knees, aware of a slight drag in his left leg. It was not important, he thought, and when he reached the path he sat down with his back against rock and kept saying:

"I'm all right. I'm perfectly all right. I'm absolutely and perfectly all right."

"Oh, my God, I'm sick," she said. "Oh, my God — I'm so sick."

"I'll hold you. Lie against the rock," he said.

But he found that he could not hold her. He lay against the rock too, trembling all over. The valley swam below him. Whole waves of dust-bright haze washed over him, drowning him in sweat, leaving him cold.

"I knew I was gone," he said. "I know what the end is like now."

"Let's go down," she said.

His eyes were shut. His sweating face seemed to be glued against a cool bone of projecting rock.

He thought the rock moved. He discovered then that it was her own face, terribly and dryly cool. His sweat was drying too and he shuddered. Then he felt the sun burning his eyeballs through lids that were like dry thin tissue and he knew that if he did not get up and walk he would slide in weakness, like a dislodged stone, off the edge of the gorge.

They were far down on the path, at the place where they had lunched, before she said:

"I never liked heights. I could never bear them. I hate that awful vertigo."

He was glad to see that Manuel had taken him at his word and had started back. He was glad too that the path was at last doubly wide, so that the two of them could walk together.

The idea that something was very wrong with his left foot came to him slowly. The drag of it was heavy and finally it woke into pain.

He found himself at last sitting on the path staring into a shoe half full of blood.

"It was all my fault," she said. "I wanted to go up there."

Half blindly he poured blood onto the dust of the path and struggled to put on his wet, blackening shoe. Somehow he could not get it back.

Nothing of the kind, he thought. He felt tired and sick. Staring at the bloodstained shoe, he remembered clearly how she had not wanted to go. He recalled his own exultation at rising above Manuel and the bird in the sky. It seemed so ridiculous now that he could only say:

"I didn't want to go either. I hate the damn place."

He sat there for a long time trying to put on his shoe. He could smell the old corrupt dark smell of blood as it dried. The shoe would not go back and there was something sinister and twisted about the swollen shape of his foot. Long before he gave up trying with the shoe he knew somehow that the foot was not going to take him home.

But now, trying to be bright about things, he said:

"They say it's an ill wind. Now you'll probably get an extra day to catch the *Alacantara.*"

She did not answer.

"You are going to catch it, aren't you?"

"Yes."

He suddenly wished that something more spectacular had happened back on the path. There was nothing very dramatic after all in cutting a slice or two out of your foot.

"I know her captain," he said. "I'll see that you get fixed up."

"I can understand if you're bitter about me," she said.

"I'm not bitter."

"You sound bitter."

"Perhaps because you kissed me up there."

Strength seemed to drain out of his body and it seemed a long time afterwards before she said:

"Kissing isn't always the start of something. In this case it was the end."

"The end of what?" he said. "Probably me."

"I've been running away from something. That's all. When you kissed me it was the end of running."

He wanted to say something like "Glad to have been of service, Miss Vane." A withering breath of burning rock blew into his face. His foot pained him violently, stabbing in sickening throbs, and he did not answer.

"You've been so sweet to me," she said. "Doing what I wanted."

"Husband," he said, "or what?"

"Husband."

"You must give him the love of a decaying shipping clerk when you get back," he said, "Miss Vane."

"He may not be there when I get back," she said. "That's the point. But I've got to try."

Savagely the heat blew into his face again and the raw weeping soreness of his foot made him sick.

"I'll bet he's a lousy —"

"You might call him that," she said. "But then that's sometimes how it is. Some men are lousy and they get under your skin. You know they're lousy and you can't help it. You can't fight them. But thanks to you — thanks to you I've got it worked out now. I can stop running and go back."

"Good God, don't thank me. That's what I'm for."

He knew it was no use. It was no good, that way of talking. His foot seemed to enlarge and burst like a bloated blister, bringing his head up with a sharp breath of pain. Above him the sky swung and quivered. A speck that might have been dust or a buzzard or just the shadow of something fell swiftly from it and cut across his sweat-locked eyes.

She saw his pain and said:

"I'll get Manuel. I'll get you back."

"Oh, God no! I can make it."

"I'll get Manuel. It's better."

He tried to watch her figure going down the path. Weakly he tried to call out to her to come back. Then he was alone and it was no use. He was a darkening, dribbling figure, undramatic and strengthless, slipping down from the rock.

The worst of it, some long time later, was the sight of Manuel, coming to take him away. The correct, oiled, subservient figure. The slight bow. The glance at the foot, the shoe that was black with blood. The cool eyes, the mouth that was so well shaped, so poised, that it might have ejected at any moment that maddening whistle:

"I told you so."

9

IT WAS MORNING, about ten o'clock, when Manuel carried him out to the waiting mules. The crushed arch of his foot might have been made of cactus thorns, each thorn a nerve beating nakedly up and down to the thump of blood. His head, like the foot, seemed to have swollen and he felt the great thudding pulse of it rocking outwards, rolling and striking the sides of the valley.

"I'm going to tie you onto the mule, sir. Just to be safe. In case you feel dizzy."

"Absolutely all right," he said. "Where's Madam?"

He could no longer call her Miss Vane. It was Madam now.

"She's just getting the last of her things. She's going to ride with you."

"She's got to catch the *Alacantara*," he said. "What about the car?"

"I'm going to telephone for it, sir. Then I'll send the hammock back from the top of the road."

"Hammock? For Christ's sake what hammock?"

"You'll be better in the hammock, sir."

He found himself shaking and swaying with sickness, impotent behind the fluttering ears of the mule, the entire valley projected before him in those strong high blue lines that were again pulsations rather than shadow.

"Much better if you let Madam push on. I can manage. Let her push on."

Presently he was aware of a slow transition of scene: rock and pine looming up, starry walls of cactus leaf dripping past, bright under springs, sunlight firing pine needles to masses of glass paper, ashy blue under a sickening sky.

Heat lay on the back of his neck, in spite of the towel Manuel had put there, like a burning stone. He wondered why there had been no attempt to escape the heat by starting earlier. Then he remembered not being able to sleep. Great rocks in the valley grating against each other. A far continuous thunder, a power-house noise, from across the plateau. Water, a stream somewhere, drowning him, dragging him under. He remembered falling down. He had walked out to the veranda, seeing Miss Vane there, in an attempt to show her that there was nothing wrong with his foot. He vividly remembered the band of paler hair across the black front of her head as she turned. He said "Hullo" and she screamed and out of the sky at the head of the valley a wing of blackness smothered him.

"The point is that the *Alacantara* is sometimes half a day earlier," he said. She was riding twenty or thirty paces in front of him. Her hair was a mass of pure black, with no other color but the outer minute sparkle of tawny fire. It was part of his sickness that his eyes saw the fires of each hair with remarkable clearness, so that he felt he could touch them with his hands.

He did in fact lift his hands from the saddle. As he did so the valley swayed. He was no longer part of it. The saddle was not there to grasp, nor the quivering head of the mule, nor her dark brilliant hair.

He was lost in emptiness and found himself crying out like a child. His mouth slobbered as he groped for air. Then the saddle was there, and the mule, and her head far off, black and unaware.

"It's like everything else," he said. "Never know where you are. A boat can be two days late. Or half a day early. You never really know."

If she was listening she showed no sign. For some moments he was under the impression that she had galloped far down the valley and disappeared. He shouted something. Masses of tree heather, growing taller now as the valley descended, broke apart and revealed her, drawn up and waiting, only a yard or two away.

"Did you say anything?" she said.

"No. All right. Perfectly all right."

"Say when you don't want to go on."

He could not check his mule. He seemed to be pitching forward, head first, down the track.

"Did you hear what I said about the *Alacantara?*"

"You mustn't worry about that."

"She may be early. She goes out on Wednesday. But

you never know — she might be in at midnight tonight. She sometimes is."

"Today is Friday," she said.

He knew that he could not have heard her correctly. He knew that it was only yesterday that he had fallen off the track. It was only an hour or two since he had emptied out his shoe, with its old sour smell of blood, like a dirty beaker.

"You probably won't get a passage for two or three weeks," he said.

She was too far away to answer, a dissolving fragment, under high sun, of pure white and pure black, like a distant road sign that was the warning of a bend.

"That's the way with this island. It's easy to get here but it's hell's own job to get away."

Some time later he was aware of the undergrowth of pine giving up a pair of stunted figures in black trilby hats. He saw the canopy of a hammock, red-flowered like an old bed coverlet between the poles. He was saying, "Let me alone. Let me walk," and then he was being lifted in. It was rather difficult lifting him in because of his leg and because only one end of the pole could be held up. The other was in the ground, leaving one man free to lift him and set him down.

It was stupid about the leg. As they took him down from the mule he could not feel it at all. Its pain had become self-numbed like the pain of a tooth at a dentist's threshold. All his pain was between his eyes, brightening his vision so that the little flowers of the hammock pattern sprang at him, dancing pink and blue with fire.

"What about you?" he said. "You push on. You've got to go. Anyway the plane is on Saturdays."

"That can wait," she said. "That isn't important. The important thing is to get you down. We ought to have done it before."

"You'd got it all so clear," he said.

The pole straightened. He was lying parallel with the sky. She wiped his face several times with a handkerchief.

"How now?" she said. "Do you feel fit to go?"

"Fit," he said. "Absolutely." And then in a moment of brightness: "Don't forget the handbag."

"I nearly would have done." His impression was that she was crying. He was not sure. She kissed him gently on the mouth and said: "Take it easy. Easy does it."

"Easy," he said. "That's what you said before."

A few moments later the trilby hats began to carry him slowly, in the hammock, down the path. Easy, he thought, that was it. How easy it had been. A ship, a handbag on a bed, a hotel, a *leste* burning through the town, a rest-house, a track to the top of the sky. Easy: that was her word.

"How do you feel?" she said. "Do you want them to go slower?"

"No," he said. "Aren't you really going now?"

"No," she said. "Not yet. Not now."

Delirium exploded a moment later in stars of pain. There was a smell of camphor from the hammock sheet, anesthetic, making him gasp for breath; and then, unexpectedly, he was aware of a strange impression.

He stared up at the sky. In the center of it he could have sworn he saw a shadow, huge and descending, in the shape of the buzzard, holding the sky in its claws.

"Easy," she said, and "Easy" his mind echoed, remembering the shape of her mouth in the sun.

The next moment he began fighting. "I won't go!" he shouted. "I won't go! I won't let it happen to me!" But she did not hear him. The trilby hats did not hear him either, and with calm slowness they carried him forward through the valley, down under the scorning brilliance of noon, towards the sea.

The Queen of Spain Fritillary

I was a dark-haired, pretty and rather tiresome girl of seventeen when my mother and elder sister took me on my first visit to a house called Orleans, a short distance above a wide bend of the river and overlooking some miles of meadows, in the Valley of the Ouse.

It was one of those rare afternoons in July when the air was drenched in the scent of roses and the fragrance of hay lying thick-cut in field after field along the river as we drove up in the big landaulet taxi we had hired to bring us from the village station. It was very hot that day, in spite of a strong breeze, and with a remarkable shimmering light on all the distances.

This light had one extraordinary effect I shall never forget. As we drove along the road to the house we were, at one point, high above the valley on an open ridge. Below us we could see perhaps a mile of river winding in big curves, under humpbacked bridges of stone, among the rich flat fields of hay.

Suddenly I saw, repeated again and again, all along the stream, what I thought at first were flocks of pure white ducks. They seemed to be floating quite motionless, between dark green banks of reed. Then, as the taxi dropped further and further down the valley, I saw that I was mistaken. What I had thought were ducks were really whole islands, purest white, of water lilies, in the crown of their bloom.

"I hope you're not going to sulk again, child," my mother said.

I had not been quite myself that summer; I was probably outgrowing my strength, my mother would tell me. It was true that I was often sulking and I must confess I felt most like sulking when my mother called me child.

It is perhaps a good thing to make it plain, also, that I did not get on at all well with my sister.

Angela was a very determined person of twenty-five, fair-haired, healthy and ambitious, who was going to be married in October. Our visit to this house, with its attractive and un-English name of Orleans, was part of a long search for somewhere where she and her fiancé, Ewart Mackeson, a successful junior partner in a leather-tanning company, could live. Mr. Ewart Mackeson was a person of ambitions too.

It was still fairly easy to get servants in those days and what Mr. Mackeson and my sister were looking for was a house of twelve or fifteen rooms, with stables if possible, an orchard or paddock, perhaps a few acres of shooting, a lawn on which to play tennis and an entrance marked TRADESMEN at the side.

Neither Angela nor Mr. Ewart Mackeson understood architecture, beauty or anything of that sort. What they were looking for was quite simple. It was, as I once told them with what I thought was a flash of enlightened sarcasm, suburbia in tweeds. Mr. Ewart Mackeson was in fact an example of a type that has become more and more common with the passing years. He wanted to be an officer in a good suburban regiment, playing the country squire.

You might have thought that that sort of house would not have been difficult to find. The country is after all full of them. It is the sort of house that used so often to be called The Grange or The Cedars or sometimes even The Towers; it almost invariably had Virginia creeper covering its red brickwork and well-kept gardens where clipped hedges of box enclosed beds of yellow calceolaria, blue lobelia and scarlet geraniums. It was a type of house — residence is really the right word — built exclusively by

and for people like Mr. Ewart Mackeson and my sister
and in a way it was, I suppose, part of the country's backbone.

There is no doubt that houses have souls, but I suppose
they reveal themselves only to certain temperaments to
which they are suited. Certainly, that summer, no house
revealed its soul to us. We must have looked at twenty or
thirty altogether and all of them hopeless. If their views
were entrancing their sanitation was primeval; if they
possessed stables they were also next to the gasworks; if
their gardens were delightful there were odors suspicious
of mice in the bedrooms.

Everyone knows, I suppose, about these impossible
characteristics of houses for sale and all I really want to
make clear is that by that hot afternoon in mid-July I had
reached the point when I never wished to see another
house. I had in fact made up my mind not to go to see
Orleans. I had somehow worked up inside myself such an
antipathy towards that house that I spent most of the
morning lying at the bottom of the garden, staring into
space, sulking.

It is only fair to say that I was very often sulking. One
of my most frequent and formidable sulks was in fact
about Mr. Ewart Mackeson. From the first Mr. Mackeson
put my back up. It is not possible to explain it easily,
but whenever he came into the room I felt myself begin
to bristle. In fact there was even more to it than that. One

of the first manifestations of my not being well that summer was a tendency to go off to my room and lie down, refusing to eat, when Mr. Mackeson came to supper. My blood curdled at the thought of him and his invasion of our three-part feminine privacy.

There was, for example, the instance of the colored leather. One of Mr. Mackeson's more enterprising business experiments was that of tanning leather in exquisite new bright shades. They were really exquisite, some of those chrome yellows, scarlets, royal blues, emeralds, lime greens and even pinks and pigeon grays. The tanning of leather is not, I suppose, a very romantic occupation except to the chemists who conjure up the dyes and it was beyond me to grasp at seventeen that Mr. Ewart Mackeson was himself a talented person, something of an artist in his way.

One evening that spring, anyway, he brought along to the house several samples of these bright new leathers to show my sister. He wanted her to choose a color — if she liked, several colors — so that he could have made for her a pair of shoes and a handbag to match them.

Finally Angela chose a pale green leather, almost the shade of an unripe bean. I did not say anything. A color can be exquisite in itself and yet be atrocious, pure murder, for a certain type of person. I knew that that pale bean shade would kill my sister's pale hair and features, but I made no comment. And then Mr. Mackeson said:

"And what about you, Mrs. Burnett? Wouldn't you like to choose something too?"

My mother was a tall pink woman who was sometimes inclined to gush. Alternatively she would simper. She, too, like my sister, was fair and pale. Although her body was angular and thin, she always wore long boned corsets and in summer carried a dark gray parasol to keep the sun from her face, with its unblemished complexion of China rose. The result was that sometimes she had the appearance of being embalmed.

"Oh, no, I couldn't, Ewart, I couldn't. I really couldn't," she said.

That was, of course, just a pose of hers; it was simply a case of protesting too much. The gush was far too obvious. And presently my mother, after more pressure from Mr. Mackeson and more refusal and more protest from her, was choosing her own piece of leather.

"That red, I think. No, the yellow. Shall I? I love the red — I do absolutely love the red. Like a tomato, isn't it? What shall it be, Angela? What do you say?"

Finally, of all things, she chose a yellow. It was a mustard yellow, unfriendly, chemical and hard. It was a hopeless color for anyone except a dark person like myself, or even a colored person, to wear.

But I still made no comment. My mother, I remember, made a few more gushing remarks about how heavenly and charming that shade of yellow was and how generous and too nice Mr. Ewart Mackeson was, and then he suddenly turned to me and said:

"Now, Laura, what about you? Come on now — what do you fancy?"

I suppose he was simply trying to be ordinarily civil and nice to me; I suppose he could hardly have done less than that. But suddenly I got up, looked witheringly at him and said with sarcasm:

"No thank you. I don't want to look like a mustard plaster. Or something in a pea-green boat for that matter," and then turned sharply on my heel and went upstairs.

The truth is that I was very fond of my sister. She was already a young woman, wearing woman's clothes, when I was eleven or twelve. I looked up to her with that distant heroine worship that only the very young can give and there was of course nothing at all to affect it or disturb it until Mr. Ewart Mackeson appeared. It was very hard for me to accustom myself, though I did not consciously grasp it at the time, that my sister was going to be taken away from me.

From all this it is easy to see why, as I sat in the back of the landaulet taxi that afternoon, staring at the river, the meadows of hay and the water lilies that looked like crowds of pure white ducks in the simmering light of July, my mother should say:

"I hope you're not going to sulk again, child, I hoped we'd got over that."

I was in fact not sulking. I was really absorbed in that illusive trick of light that the afternoon had played on me. I was really entranced by the fact that a crowd of ducks had turned themselves into water lilies and I wanted to be left alone with the idea, entranced, for a little longer.

That was why I said, as the taxi drew up at the iron gates of the house, under a long row of tall, flowering limes:

"I'm not coming in. I'll sit here and wait for you."

"I shall not argue," my mother said. She got out of the car and snapped up her dark gray parasol. "I shall not argue. There's no point in wasting breath. As long as you behave like a child you must be treated as a child."

I wanted to point out, tensely, that I was not a child. Instead I said:

"I might even start to walk back. You can pick me up on the way."

"Do entirely as you wish," my mother said. "Have it entirely your own way."

A minute later she disappeared with my sister up the gravel drive, between thick shrubberies of lilac and laurustinus, towards the stone white-windowed house that could be seen, with its high white doorway and its big black iron boot-scraper, at the end.

Presently I heard the doorbell ring. After a few moments I saw an elderly maid in white cap and apron answer the door. Then my mother and sister disappeared

into the house and after that I suppose I sat there for
four or five minutes before I became aware of an extraordinary thing.

I suddenly experienced an overwhelming curiosity about
the house. I felt that I had to see it after all. It was not
simply that it was in itself very different from all those
Virginia-creepered, half-towered desirable residences we
had seen all summer. It was not simply because it had no
Virginia creeper to smother the walls. It was true that it
had a big pale yellow rose, with almost plum-colored foli-
age, growing above the door, and over one gable one of
those huge magnolias, with thick polished leaves, whose
flowers are so like large pure cream chalices when they
open in late hot summers.

All these things were attractive in themselves but they
had nothing to do with what I had started to feel. What I
felt had nothing particularly to do with beauty, with the
charm of the yellow rose above the doorway, the flowerless magnolia cool in the heat or the drenching fragrance
of the long row of limes. It had nothing to do, either, with
that curious sensation people so often experience with
places, and with houses especially: the sensation, not
always pleasant and sometimes uncannily disturbing, that
they have been there before.

What I felt was a rather startling sense of communica-
tion with that house. Of course the sensory impressions
and perception of the very young are often overacute and

perhaps the definition of what I felt may sound absurd. But this is the way youth feels and it did not seem at all absurd to me that afternoon that the house had, as it were, something to say to me. That is perhaps a naïve and clumsy way of putting it and the only other way I can express it is to say that it was rather like your being in a room and hearing urgent whispers of conversation going on in another.

In a situation like that you are more than eaten up with overwhelming curiosity. You realize that if you don't listen at that moment, quickly, it will be too late. You will never know what the urgent whispers of conversation are about. It will all be lost and you will regret it forever.

That was why, a few moments later, I was walking up the drive.

I rang the doorbell twice, but nothing happened. I discovered afterwards that there was only one servant indoors and that she at that moment was showing my mother and my sister through the rooms upstairs.

After another two or three minutes I decided not to ring again and I started to walk back down the drive. And then, for the second time, I experienced that extraordinary feeling of curiosity. And almost at once, not stopping to think, I turned and began to walk round to the side of the house, through a large archway of yew, into the gardens beyond.

The gardens sloped away sharply, in a series of terraces joined by stone steps, to the river. I was surprised to see them, in contrast to the front of the house, running wild. Tall coarse yellow mulleins, with caterpillar-eaten leaves, had sown themselves all through the flower beds, among the roses and even, at one place, in broken cucumber frames. Sunflowers were presently going to obliterate the beds of asparagus. Soon there would be nothing to be seen of a plantation of raspberries, struggling with an invasion of white convolvulus in full trumpet bloom.

I walked slowly through this choking mass of vegetation to the river. A path ran along the bank, heavily shaded by big balsam poplar trees. You could smell the fragrance of balsam leaves in the hot flat air and in the shadow of the trees the river was dark, with deep underskeins of weed.

Halfway along the path was a little wooden landing stage with a seat on it. It was surrounded by a handrail and a punt was chained to the end. The punt, the little seat, the landing stage and in fact everything about it were, unlike the garden, surprisingly well kept. The punt had recently been painted a fresh bright green and even the name of the house, Orleans, had been picked out in white at the stern end.

I followed the path for forty or fifty yards along the

river and began presently to approach the boundaries of the garden on the other side. It was wilder than ever there, with a few straggling pyramid pear trees growing in long meadow grass as tall as wheat and in full seed.

Beyond all this was another hedge of yew, ten or twelve feet high, with a path cut through the grass beside it. I started to walk up this path. Then, halfway up the slope, I heard a voice. It was a man's voice and it seemed, I thought, to be talking to itself in the hot still air.

And it was talking very remarkably. I am not sure at this distance of time if I can remember word for word exactly what it was saying but presently what I heard was, I think, something like this:

"It forms a ladder of its web so that it can climb up it to any height — even up a pane of glass. They smell awfully disagreeable but apparently the Romans thought them delicious. They were a favorite dish of theirs."

That was about all I heard before I came upon the man himself, standing by the hedge. He was a man of sixty or so, a little under medium height, rather spruce, with very smooth gray hair. He was wearing a cream shantung summer jacket, gray trousers with a chalk stripe in them and a white panama.

There was nothing in the least remarkable about all this. What was remarkable was that he was holding a branch of about half a dozen leaves in his hand. At first I thought he was talking to these leaves. Then I saw that I was mistaken. Something was crawling up the branch and I concluded, mistakenly as it turned out, that he was talking to that.

It was a thick, pink, naked, quite repulsive caterpillar.

If it is surprising for a girl of seventeen to come upon an elderly gentleman in a strange garden talking to an ugly caterpillar it must be equally surprising for elderly gentlemen to have conferences of this kind interrupted by strange girls of seventeen.

The surprising thing was that he did not show surprise at all. He looked at me, then looked at the caterpillar, which had now reached the tip of the branch, and seemed for a moment undecided which of us to attend to first. Then, very deftly, he turned the branch the other way up, so that the caterpillar could climb up it again, and with the other hand raised his panama.

As he took off his hat I saw that his eyes, remarkably blue in the brilliant sunshine, transfixed me.

"Good afternoon," he said.

I began to explain how it was I was there, how sorry I was to interrupt him and so on, and he said, "Yes. Oh, yes! Yes, of course," several times, watching me with the remarkably bright blue eyes while I in turn stood watching the caterpillar.

"Will this lead me back to the house?" I said.

"One moment. One moment," he said and then started to address the hedge:

"It seems I have visitors. About the house. You understand, dear, don't you? I'll show you a figure of the goat later. It's rather a treasure. This one's a bit of a freak of course. He ought not to be out now. He ought to have been out in May, but that's how it is sometimes."

Of course youth is very quick to spot the ridiculous. And suddenly I thought I'd never seen anything quite as killing as the business of holding this repulsive caterpillar on a stick and carrying on a two-part conversation with it and a hedge. It seemed funnier still when, through a break in the hedge, I saw the flap of a big pink sun hat on the other side and heard a woman's voice say:

"Of course, dear. That I shall look forward to immensely. Au revoir, Frederick. Good-by."

"Au revoir," he said.

Already by this time the caterpillar had climbed to the top of the branch and now the man in the panama, turning to me, deftly twisted the branch upside down so that the caterpillar could climb up it again.

"Do come this way," he said.

To my surprise he began to lead me back down the path, towards the river. All the time he held the branch at half arm's length, rather like a torch, and I didn't think I'd ever see anything quite so fatuous.

As if to make the whole thing more ridiculous he seemed absolutely absorbed in me. He talked very quickly, in rather a fluty sort of voice, asking all sorts of questions.

Then, unable to take his eyes off me, he eventually completely forgot the caterpillar, which finally reached the top of the stick and sat there looking most disagreeably naked and slightly bloated.

"So you've come to see this house?" he said. "Well, well. How nice. Indeed. How nice. These are the only two houses that front on the river here. All the rest of the land, you see, is meadow. With a continual danger of floods, you see, so that you can't build down there. It's only just here, because of this bend and the big bank, that it's been possible to have these houses."

It was, I still thought, extraordinarily funny: the prattling fluty voice, the enthusiasm, the eagerness, like that of a boy, and always, of course, the caterpillar.

And presently the caterpillar itself got funnier still. At the path by the river we stopped for nearly five minutes while he went into a prolonged explanation about the punt and the landing stage. By this time I was not listening very closely and he, more and more absorbed in me, was not looking at the caterpillar.

I saw that it had, in fact, crawled back down the stick and now, slowly and steadily, hunching its back, was crawling up his arm.

"And what is your name? I mean," he said, "your Christian name."

"Laura," I said.

"How charming," he said. The little bright blue eyes glittered, dancing with pleasure as the caterpillar crawled up the neat shantung arm. "And what are you? I mean how old? Seventeen?"

"Nineteen," I said.

The whole affair was so ridiculous that the lie about my age was, I thought, not only in keeping with it all but made it, if possible, more fun.

"Still at school?"

"Oh, heavens no!" I said. And this time I didn't lie. "I haven't been to school all summer."

"No?" he said. "Well, you don't look like a schoolgirl. You look too sure of yourself for that."

I suppose that flattered me: to be told that I looked as old as I had pretended to be. But even the flattery didn't quite cancel out the comic tone of the whole situation. The caterpillar was now, I saw, crawling on his shoulder. I watched it, fascinated, ready to shriek if it reached his neck.

He, on the other hand, didn't seem to notice it at all and presently he said, tapping the little seat on the landing stage:

"Come and sit down for a minute and tell me all about yourself."

"I ought to go," I said. I began to explain how my mother and my sister would be waiting for me. I said something about their thinking, perhaps, that I might be walking back along the road and he said:

"Who has really come to look at the house? Your mother?"

"Oh, no, my sister. You see, she's to be married soon."

The caterpillar had reached the lapel of his shantung jacket, just above the buttonhole. It was arching its head this way and that, feeling the air.

"Is your sister like you?"

"She's fair," I said. "Like my mother. I am like my father's side."

The caterpillar decided to start its upward journey towards his neck.

Then I felt I must ask him a question.

"It's such a nice house. Are you going far away?"

"You're almost the first people to have seen it," he said. "A man did come last Sunday. A stockbroker. From Bedford. Do sit down." He tapped the seat again. "But I've heard no more. Do you know France?" he said.

He moved along the seat. Skirts were a great deal shorter in those days and I fancied he looked quickly at my legs as I sat down. I thought they were very nice legs and I was glad he seemed to think so too.

"No," I said. "I don't know France. I've never been abroad."

I suppose the fact that I was watching the caterpillar with such unbroken fascination must have misled him into thinking I was staring solely at him. At any rate the bright blue eyes were continually holding mine in a shimmering, captivated smile.

"I used to live a great deal in France," he said. "Before the war. Then I came and took this place. But I find the winters very cold in this valley."

The caterpillar, I noticed, had disappeared.

"Must you go?" he said.

By that time I had really begun to enjoy the whole situation. It appealed enormously to my sense of humor to see that fat bald creature crawling all over him and now disappearing, at last, behind his neck.

"No. I suppose I don't have to," I said. "They'll wait for me."

"Good," he said. "Now you can tell me more about yourself."

It was beautifully dark and cool there on the riverbank, under the thick poplars, and when a fish rose, just on the line of shadow, it cut the water with a curved slice of silver before it disappeared.

That was about the only thing that moved in the hot breathless afternoon for the next quarter of an hour, during which he said once:

"Tell me. I've really been most undecided about this

house. I'm really very fond of it. But I can't exist in these freezing winters. If this were your house what would you do?"

"Do you live alone?" I said.

I don't know what made me say that. I suppose it's instinctive in any woman, as soon as a man appears on the scene, to try to assess whether he has attachments or not. I don't know of course. It may not have been that. At any rate he said:

"That's another thing. I hardly see a soul from one week's end to another. Except Miss Carfax. She lives in the house next door."

"Was that Miss Carfax you were talking to?"

"That was Miss Carfax."

Again I started to search his neck for the caterpillar. It was absolutely fascinating to wonder where it could have got to all that time and I must have been so absorbed that I couldn't have realized fully how much my eyes were fixed on him.

"But let's not talk," he said, "about Miss Carfax."

Suddenly I got the impression that, with the slightest encouragement from me, he would have become emotional. His bright eyes fairly shimmered, like the heat of the afternoon.

A moment later I saw the caterpillar emerge on the other side of his coat collar.

I started laughing at once and he said:

"You're a very gay person, aren't you? Are you always so gay?"

"It doesn't always do to be serious, does it?" I said and because of the caterpillar I was still laughing.

All this, of course, may well have looked like a form of encouragement to him and suddenly he moved along the seat, a little closer to me.

But then, instead of attempting to come any nearer, he merely patted my hand. It was a very brief, avuncular sort of pat, not very serious, but I drew my hand away a little haughtily and with the faintest smile. I was really thinking more of the caterpillar on my own arms and shoulders and I did not grasp, even remotely, that this quick little pat of my hand was really an expression of great shyness on his part.

I suppose youth never thinks of age as being shy. It merely thinks that a person of sixty ought long since to have got over things like that. It is in fact impossible for the young to grasp that the pain of shyness never really leaves some people, however age may seem to give them certainty.

That, anyway, was the one and only attempt he made to pat my hand and presently he said:

"It must be rather interesting to have two fair people and two dark ones in the family. Your mother and sister on the one side and you and your father on the other."

"My father is dead," I said.

His comment on that was, as I afterwards discovered, quite typical.

"Do you miss him very much?" he said.

"Very much," I said. "Naturally."

That was another thing I had not, at that time, fully grasped. My father had died the previous summer. Shortly afterwards my sister had got engaged to Ewart Mackeson. It did not occur to me that these two events had anything to do with that sulky adolescent sickness of mine.

"Are you on the telephone?" he suddenly said.

"Yes," I said. "Why?"

"If I sell the house I might perhaps give a little farewell party before I go away. If I do I would like to ring you up and invite you. Would you care to come?"

"Thank you," I said.

In thought he stared at the water, still holding the branch of leaves, and I could not see the caterpillar. I still longed for it to complete the picture of fatuity by crawling up his neck, but a moment later I thought I heard voices from the direction of the mullein-strewn wilderness nearer the house, and soon they were growing louder.

"I think my mother and sister must be coming this way," I said.

Suddenly I saw that the caterpillar had appeared again. It was sitting on the far lapel of the shantung coat.

"You haven't answered my question," he said.

That is the sort of opening youth likes and I said at once, with what I thought was splendid sarcasm:

"Since you ask me a new one every five seconds it's rather hard to know which question you mean."

"About the house."

Up to that moment I simply couldn't have cared one way or the other whether he sold the house or not. What on earth had I to do with the wretched house? Then from farther up the bank I distinctly heard my sister say:

"I think Ewart will rave about it, don't you? All this bit by the river. I must get him over tomorrow."

I didn't hesitate a moment longer. I simply turned and smiled at him in a calm offhand sort of way and said:

"If you mean about selling the house I wouldn't sell it for worlds. Nothing would induce me."

I thought he seemed relieved at that, almost delighted. He actually gave me a fussy little pat on the shoulder.

"I hope you will come over to tea with me one day," he said, "while this beautiful weather lasts. I would love to show you the butterflies."

I simply couldn't think what on earth he was talking about. He murmured something else about not really wanting, in his heart, to part with the house and how glad he was about my turning up that day and helping him to make up his mind, and then my sister and mother arrived.

He went towards them and, still with the caterpillar sitting on his chest, gave a little bow, at the same time raising his panama.

"I have been talking to your charming daughter without knowing her name or telling her mine," he said. "I'm Frederick Fielding-Brown. Good afternoon."

"Mrs. George Burnett," my mother said. "Good afternoon," and I saw her suddenly look with pale startled eyes at the extraordinary spectacle of the shantung jacket and its naked caterpillar.

"I should like to bring my fiancé over to see the house," my sister said. "I love it."

My sister, seeing the caterpillar too, looked equally startled.

"By all means," he said, "though to be perfectly honest I haven't really made up my mind finally whether to sell it or not."

Back in the car my sister was half irritated, half amused.

"Stupid little man," she said. "First he wants to sell his house and then he can't make up his mind. And did you ever see anything quite so priceless? That revolting caterpillar on his coat — did you see that caterpillar?"

I could only stare out of the taxi window and down the valley to where, on the river, the water lilies were gleaming as white, entrancing and ducklike as ever in the sun.

"I didn't see anything," I said, "and if it comes to that I don't think he was stupid. I think he was rather nice. He was very charming to me."

Two days later my mother was congratulating me on having at last had the good sense, as she put it, to shake myself out of myself.

"A bicycle ride will do you all the good in the world," she said. "I can't think why you haven't taken to it before. Would you like me to pack you some tea?"

"No thank you," I said. "I'll stop in a village somewhere and get some."

An hour later I was sitting in the drawing room at Orleans, taking tea with Frederick Fielding-Brown. The afternoon was hot and brilliant. The yellow Venetian blinds were drawn halfway down at the windows. There was a strong scent of lilies in the air.

"I didn't think you would come over so soon after my letter," he said.

Youth is not always sarcastic and sharp and quick to see the comic side of things. Sometimes it is splendidly tactless too.

"I hadn't anything else to do," I said, "so I thought I'd just come over."

He was very tolerant about that. He smiled and asked me to help myself to tomato sandwiches. They were, I thought, very good tomato sandwiches, with rather a special flavor to them. I remarked on this flavor and felt that

I was being clever when I told him I thought they were piquant.

"That's because I have a tiny touch of mayonnaise and red pepper put on them," he said. "How observant you are."

He started to pour tea from a conical silver pot, afterwards filling up the pot with hot water from a little silver spirit kettle.

"I don't suppose you've ever eaten caterpillars of any sort, have you?" he said.

Here we were, I thought, back in the madhouse. It was obviously going to be too screamingly funny for words.

Then he began to explain. He started to remind me of the day I had first found him in the garden, talking to the caterpillar, Miss Carfax and the hedge.

"That was a caterpillar of the goat moth," he said. "It seems the Romans ate them. Considered them quite a delicacy. I suppose in the category of frogs and snails. Or grasshoppers perhaps. What they ate them with is another matter."

"Perhaps mayonnaise," I said.

There was nothing, I thought, like playing up on these occasions.

"Well, and why not?" he said. "I suppose if you were brought up on *Cossus ligniperda* and mayonnaise you would think no more of it, in the end, than eating winkles with vinegar and a pin."

"What is *Cossus ligniperda?*"

"That," he said, "is the goat moth."

Once or twice before and after this lunatic piece of conversation he remarked on what a charming companion I was and how glad he was that I had been able to come over.

"You are wearing such a pretty dress," he said. "It goes well with your dark complexion."

"Thank you," I said.

The dress was a bright clear green, lighter and softer than emerald, with short, yellow-trimmed sleeves and a yellow collar. With it I was wearing the yellow shoes that Ewart Mackeson had made for my mother. She didn't like them after all and now, in consequence, I thought they were rather smart on me.

"What material is it?" he said. He fingered one of the sleeves. His hand brushed my bare upper arm and drew away. "A kind of silk?"

I said I thought it was rayon. By this time, however, he was looking at my shoes. He seemed entranced by them too and he peered at them a long time with absorbed brilliant blue eyes.

"You have wonderful taste," he said, "to get shoes to match like that."

This was, as best as I can give it, the general tone of the afternoon. It was poised somewhere between lunacy

and flattery, with a curious overtone of charm. The way
he poured tea for me, helped me to sandwiches and finally
to dish after dish of large dark ruby strawberries completely immersed in cream — all these things were, I suppose, quite enough to counteract, for a young girl with a
fairly high opinion of herself and her beauty, a feeling
that she was simply the guest of a hopeless eccentric
who didn't know what day it was.

I never intended, of course, to pay another visit. That
would have been too much. The idea of striking up a
friendship with an elderly man who seriously thought
that goat moths and mayonnaise were a solemn gastronomic possibility was altogether too ludicrous for words.

And it is possible, I think, that I never should have
paid another visit if it had not been for an incident that
occurred after tea was over and I suddenly got up, now
rather bored by that stuffy yellow-shaded drawing room
and its too oppressive fragrance of Madonna lilies, and
said that I ought to go.

"Oh, no, please! I want you to meet Miss Carfax," he
said. "Miss Carfax is coming over."

The life of Frederick Fielding-Brown and that of Miss
Carfax were, as I was to discover later, about as ludi-
crously bound up with each other as he himself was with
the business of moths and butterflies.

Every Wednesday afternoon, for example, Frederick

Fielding-Brown handed in his card to the house next door and formally went to tea with Miss Carfax; every Sunday afternoon Miss Carfax handed in her card at his house and took tea with him. During the rest of the week they corresponded with each other by a series of daily notes taken to each house by hand, in his case by the garden boy, in hers by the chauffeur.

These notes pulsated warmly with urgent and stunning discoveries in the world of entomology. Sometimes they were accompanied, in Miss Carfax's case, by little perforated cardboard boxes.

"Is it treasure?" she would write. "I trust so. I found it in the raspberry canes."

In a return note he would tell her that her treasure was, after all, no more than a Painted Lady, a Red Admiral, a Tortoiseshell or something of that sort, common to all our counties.

Miss Carfax was, however, never discouraged. Tending her garden, snipping at rambler roses, walking along meadow paths, by the river, she kept up a great vigilance for things that would interest him, secretly hoping that she would one day come upon something of rare and stupefying importance, such as a Feathered Prominent, a Purple Emperor or a Brixton Beauty.

In turn he wrote notes of discoveries whose detection she apparently found to be nothing short of magical.

There would be illuminating occasions like those of the goat moth, which had made me laugh so much, or the woolly case-bearer, a moth of which, as he explained to me and no doubt also to Miss Carfax, the virgin females sometimes lay fruitful eggs.

The way in which these two elderly people twittered backwards and forwards to each other's houses, taking tea, writing notes, exchanging larvae and so on, prattling passionately through the garden hedge, tremulous with discovery, was of course just the thing that a young girl would find amusing and fatuous. For the life of me I simply couldn't, I'm afraid, see what all the fuss was for.

That was why I thought Miss Carfax looked quite pathetic, almost imbecile with excitement, as she came rushing into the drawing room that afternoon, carrying with trembling care a little cardboard box, saying:

"I really think I have something, Frederick, I really think I've something for you at last."

I ought to explain that, just before this happened, he had been trying to persuade me to come to tea another day. We were sitting on a narrow sofa. It was in a kind of French marquetry style and it was too high for comfort. It reminded me very much of the seat by the river and once again he started patting my hands.

"Come again, will you? While this beautiful weather lasts? Do you like raspberries?"

If you can imagine an elderly man shyly patting your hand, looking intensely into your eyes and saying, "Do you like raspberries?" you will know something of what I felt that afternoon just before Miss Carfax burst in.

Then he said:

"Come early. We'll take the punt on the river. We'll go down to where the water lilies are."

Suddenly, at the mention of water lilies, I felt quite differently about the whole affair. He seemed to me suddenly very sweet, in that avuncular attentive way of his; he was full of eager, tender charm.

"I should love to see the water lilies," I said. "From the road they look like ducks —"

"Then you will?" he said. "You —"

I hadn't time to answer before the maid was knocking on the door and, a moment later, showing Miss Carfax into the room.

"I really think I have something —"

Her hands fluttered, but I noticed that he did not seem to be looking either at them or at the little box they were holding. Instead he gave me an engaging, pitying little smile — pitying, that is, for Miss Carfax, who was so absorbed in taking the lid off the box that she didn't even know I was there.

"My dear," he said gently, "allow me to introduce Miss Burnett. Miss Carfax — Miss Burnett."

In her fluttering struggle with the box Miss Carfax

managed to acknowledge me with a kind of unsmiling grin. I ought to have explained that she was of course old too — that is, fifty-six or fifty-seven I should say — with long angular teeth, straight as piano keys.

"There!" she said. "There!"

"Miss Burnett and I have had a most delightful tea together," he said. "I'm sure we ate more strawberries than were good for us, but some things are irresistible when the season's so short —"

"Look," she said. "Look, Frederick. Please look, will you?"

He was, during all this time, looking at me. Now he gave a cursory glance at the box, just in time to see a large brown-pink moth fly upwards, towards the light, and attach itself to one of the Venetian blinds.

"Oh! It's gone! — It's out —"

"Why don't you use the cyanide I gave you?" he said sharply. "Either that or keep the lid on."

Her eyes seemed to give a pained gray jolt as he said this. Her hands flapped helplessly and she said:

"Can we catch it? What kind is it, Frederick? It's so huge. I thought it might be a Great Brocade —"

He laughed and it seemed to stun her. She stood mute in the middle of the room.

"I'm surprised," he said. "I'm really surprised at you, dear. I think even Miss Burnett would know our common Privet Hawk."

Soon, after all her excitement, she seemed to become slack and baggy. She sat down and we talked a bit. I can't think what about — more moths, I think, and how good the strawberries were. I could see, however, that she was never really listening. Her bemused eyes wandered sometimes to where the moth was folded on the Venetian blinds and sometimes she sucked at her big teeth and swallowed hard so that her Adam's apple quivered.

Then, after she had gone, he actually laughed at her. "A Great Brocade," he said. "If she lives to be a hundred she'll never find a Great Brocade."

Then I said what I suppose was rather a foolish thing.

"That doesn't give her very much time, does it?"

Of course that was clever and quick and I must say he absolutely loved it too. "Most amusing," he said. "But naughty. Very naughty."

"Well," I said, "isn't it nice to be naughty sometimes?"

It was that, I suppose, that set the tone for the rest of the afternoon and the future. We sat on the little sofa again and he squeezed my hand. His fingers were hot and sticky. Then I crossed my legs and pulled my skirt down over my knees and he said:

"What about tea again? Which day? We'll have masses of raspberries and cream and go to see the water lilies afterwards."

"Which day would you like me to come?"

"Whichever day you wish," he said. "All days are your days. Tomorrow — Friday, Saturday, Sunday — they're all yours. Just say."

"Sunday," I said.

So, without thinking, I went over again on Sunday. It was a warm breezy afternoon and we ate many dishes of raspberries for tea — very special, beautiful yellow ones, I remember, as well as the ordinary red kind — and afterwards, as he had promised, we took the punt and paddled slowly down the river to where the water lilies were.

Perhaps it was the warm sleepy wind, perhaps it was the sight of occasional pairs of lovers lying in the long grasses by the waterside, or it may have been merely that funny, sensuous sort of feeling that floating on water gives you — I don't know, but that afternoon I began to lead him on a little, just for fun.

"You look very hot, paddling all the time," I said once. "Why don't we tie up the punt for a while?"

So we tied up the punt and got out and I lay down on the riverbank in the tall whitening August grasses. They were so high, these grasses, as high as oats and almost the same gold-white ripe color, with bowed feathery heads of seed, that they made a wall round me where I lay on my back, staring at the sky.

Before long, as I lay there, he leaned over and, for the first time, kissed me. I didn't mind very much; nor was I very excited — that, I suppose, describes it fairly accurately. If a man of sixty wanted to kiss me on a hot July afternoon I thought that, on the one hand, it was silly to be prim about it. On the other hand it wasn't an experience that I'd have sought deliberately as a means of pleasure.

At the same time some pretense of approval or disapproval had to be made and I said:

"Naughty. You know that was very naughty, don't you?"

"You're so very lovely," he said. "So absolutely lovely."

"Flatterer."

He started to try to kiss me again, but this time I bit my lips and made a face at him.

"You're not eating strawberries and raspberries now," I said, "and taking second helpings. It's not good for you."

"But I feel it's rather like that," he said. "I feel the season might be so short."

"Oh?" I said. "And who said the season might be short?"

Like that I teased and taunted him for the rest of the afternoon. It was great fun altogether. Sometimes I refused to let him kiss me for a quarter of an hour or twenty minutes at a time and then it was marvelous to see how terribly downcast he was. Then I would pretend I wanted to go home and he would start protesting in awful dismay until I teased him another way and laughed in his face and said:

"I might as well go home as lie here and do nothing. I thought you wanted to kiss me so much? Goodness, you don't even try."

In that way, playing and kissing in the grasses, we spent the rest of the afternoon. By the time we paddled back to the house he was in a sort of daze. He had the air of a man in a mild state of intoxication. I felt a little heady too — warm from lying in the sun in breezy meadows, from the smell of water and meadowsweet, and with grains of grass seed in my hair.

Probably that was why neither of us saw Miss Carfax until the punt was actually turning round under the balsam poplars, towards the landing stage.

"Isn't that Miss Carfax?" I said.

She was standing in the shade of the river path, in a white sun hat, staring towards us. When she saw us she turned sharply on her heel and fairly bolted away.

"Where?" he said. "Where?"

"She's gone now," I said. "She just opened her gate and disappeared."

"Oh, my God!" he said suddenly. "I just remembered. She always comes to tea with me on Sundays."

After that I suppose I went over to the house perhaps another dozen times or more. Twice I went to dinner. The great thing was, of course, that it took me out of myself. It was fun. I wasn't bored or sulky any more.

The second time I went to dinner it was already September. The mild misty evenings were drawing in. The weather was soft and humid. There were mushrooms in the meadows. I mention this because, earlier that evening, we actually went down to the fields and gathered mushrooms which were afterwards served on toast, as a savory. After that we ate pears for dessert, the lovely Marie Louise variety, peeling the smooth red skin with little pearl-handled silver knives.

"September is a good month for moths," he said. "Would you like to go out after dinner and see what we can find?"

So presently we were walking with a torch through the mullein wilderness, past the choked raspberry canes. He stood quite still once or twice, steadily shining the torch into the darkness under fruit boughs. A desultory moth or two began to dance in the light and he said:

"I didn't bring the cyanide bottle. It's hardly worth it. Mostly what you can see are common *Noctuae*."

Soon I thought he seemed nervous. He kept switching on the torch and then suddenly putting it off again. One moment the air was dancing with a crowd of small light wings and the next I was groping, half blinded, for the path among the grasses.

Suddenly he put out the light for the sixth or seventh time, stopped abruptly and took me by the shoulders.

"I want to ask you to marry me," he said. His hands were shaking dreadfully. "Will you? I know there is a great difference — but would you? Would you consider it please?"

I simply wanted to laugh outright at him.

"Now I see," I told him, "what moth it was you hoped to find out here. The rare nocturnal Laura, eh?"

Nervously he started panting, breathing hard.

"No," he said. "No. It's simply — well, I've been trying to say this for some time. Would you? Would you marry me?"

"It's very sweet of you, but —"

"Would you think it over? Think it over and give me an answer another day?"

It was quite ludicrous; he was breathing hard on me, as if blowing on a hot potato.

"Oh, no, really," I started to say. "Thank you, but —" After all, what sort of encouragement had I given him to get him to the point of asking me this?

"You've kissed me very often. You've given me such a lot of pleasure," he said. "It's been six weeks since you kissed me that Sunday afternoon —"

"Yes, but kissing —" I said — "Kissing is kissing and there's a great deal of difference between kissing and getting married. You're old enough to know that."

"Yes, but you see I don't know." He sounded sad and

dithering. "I don't know. I don't know about these things."

"Then," I teased him, "it's time you learned." Suddenly, in a way, I felt sorry for him. I linked my arm in his and we started to walk back to the house. He did not shine the torch any more. He seemed to have forgotten it. I simply felt him groping forward intensely in the September darkness.

"I'm so fond of you. I love you so much," he said. "I can't explain how much I love you."

"Yes and I'm fond of you," I said. "But —"

"I'm old, I know," he said. "I'm too old for you. Isn't that it?"

"It isn't that," I said and suddenly I arrived again at another of youth's splendid moments of tactfulness. "After all I'm only seventeen and I've got my life to think of —"

"Seventeen?" he said. "You told me you were nineteen. You see, I was thinking that if you were nineteen it wouldn't be long before you came of age. The difference wouldn't seem so great then —"

"Seventeen," I said. "I was just teasing you."

He was absolutely silent for the rest of the way back to the house. We had hardly arrived there before the maid, Mabel, came in with a note on a silver salver.

"With Miss Carfax's compliments, sir," she said.

He read the note, crumpled it up and threw it in the fireplace.

"Miss Carfax is going away for a few days," he said, "and thinks I ought to know." He took my hands and held them in his, together. "Good-by, my dear. I don't suppose you'll be coming to see me again, will you? After this?"

"Oh, good gracious," I said, "why not? Of course I'm coming to see you. That's if you ever ask me."

"Ask you?" he said. "Oh, my God, ask you?" and presently in that awfully sweet nervous way of his he was kissing my hands.

Five days later I went over to see him on the last visit I ever made.

It began to rain sharply and heavily that afternoon as I bicycled the last mile or so to the house. By the time I arrived my dress, my stockings and my hair were soaking.

"You must go up at once and take a bath," he said, "and put on a dressing gown. You mustn't catch cold whatever you do. Mabel will dry your things. Come down when you've finished and hot tea and toast will be ready."

There is a wonderful sensation of luxury about taking a hot bath on a dull afternoon with rain streaming down on the windows outside, but I am not sure it is not equaled by putting on, afterwards, a more luxurious dressing gown than you yourself own. It was probably because of this that I spent a long time over that bath and afterwards drying and brushing and setting my hair. All this time the rain streamed down on the windows and it must have been nearly five o'clock by the time I went downstairs.

I forgot to say, by the way, how full that house was of moths and butterflies. Mostly they were kept in special mahogany cabinets with long sliding drawers. But they were also mounted, separately or in small selected groups, in glass-covered cases that hung about the walls like pictures. I used sometimes to ask if he hadn't every single native species among all the hundreds that lay in the drawers and hung on the walls and up the stairs, but he would say:

"Well, no, not quite every one. You see I make it a point of honor only to mount those I've collected myself. You can buy specimens of the rarest things of course but it really isn't the same. The thrill isn't there."

As I went downstairs that afternoon, wearing the heavy silk dressing gown he had lent me, I stopped once or twice to look at the cases hanging all down the walls on either side of the stairs. I think they were mostly common species that hung there but even among the commonest there are some of the most beautiful and I was looking at a group of meadow browns I hadn't seen before when, from the drawing room, I suddenly heard voices.

It was not only because the door was open a little but because the voices had begun slightly to raise their pitch that I heard them more clearly as I came to the foot of the stairs.

"It's merely a point of honor with me, that's all," I heard him say.

"You mean you won't accept it?" It was Miss Carfax speaking and her voice was sharp and thin. "Is that it?"

"My dear —"

"Or is it just that you won't accept it from me? Perhaps that's it?"

"Not at all," he said. "It's simply that I never mount —"

"You do know what it is, I suppose, don't you?" she said. Her voice was growing tauter. "You've hardly even looked at it."

"Of course I know what it is," he said. "It's a Queen of Spain Fritillary."

"Is it rare? I heard you say once —"

"It's rare in this country," he said, "but not in France. I had scores of specimens in France but when the war came I left them there."

"I heard you say once you hadn't got one," she said. "I remembered the name so well. I thought the name was so beautiful. Now it seems you had hundreds. Well, scores —"

"But not British," he said. "A British specimen —"

"This is British!" she said. "That is the whole point of it! I understand that!" Her voice was rising towards breaking pitch, thin with anger. "I took great care about that —

that was why I bought it for you. Don't you understand? It was just a little present I thought I should like to bring back for you —"

At that moment she opened the door. I heard him begin to say, "Look, my dear. I appreciate all that. That I appreciate —" when she turned and saw me standing in the hallway outside.

For a moment or two she couldn't speak. Her mouth opened itself and stuck there in a stiff long-toothed gap, painfully ludicrous and paralyzed.

Behind her Frederick Fielding-Brown appeared and began to say, "Miss Burnett got caught in the rain —" and then got no further. She suddenly turned and gave a sort of hysterical hiss into his face. It was the sort of sound that cats make when they spit at each other and then she shouted:

"I wonder if you're quite so particular about accepting what she has to give you? Do you make that a point of honor, I wonder?"

The front door slammed. It was all so innocent on my part, my being there in the dressing gown, that I wanted to howl with laughter. How absolutely and madly idiotic the old could make themselves look, I thought, and then I saw that Frederick Fielding-Brown, still clutching the handle of the drawing room door, was white and shaking.

"Come and sit down," he said. "That has upset me." His voice was quite sepulchral. "She came just as tea arrived. Now we must ring for more toast. Would you ring?" he asked me. "My hands are shaking. The toast is cold."

It was nearly a week later when my mother, after supper, sat reading the local evening paper. My sister and Ewart Mackeson had at last found themselves a suitable house in which to live. It was nicely gabled, with much ivy growing on the walls, an important-looking coachhouse with a weathercock, an acre or two of rabbit shooting, a tradesman's entrance and a tennis court. My sister was quite crazy about the tennis court and the prospect of giving garden parties there and every evening now she and Ewart Mackeson would be over at the house, measuring it for carpets and curtains.

"Wasn't that house called Orleans?" my mother said. "The one we went to see?"

"Yes," I said.

"An awful thing has happened," she said, "if that's the same house. Was that gentleman's name Carfax? Didn't he live there with his sister?"

"No," I said. "His name was Fielding-Brown."

"That's right. Then it is the same," she said. "It's here. Listen. It says that a Miss Gertrude Carfax was found dead by the river there last Sunday and that her body was first discovered by her friend and neighbor from Orleans, the residence next door."

Before I could say anything my mother began to read

the coroner's report. "Cyanide," she said. "How dreadful. What a dreadful thing. How awful. With cyanide."

I stayed in my room for several days after that, in what my mother said was one of my old, inexplicable, maddening fits of sulking.

"If you are going to start that again," she said, "I warn you that I won't put up with it. You will go and stay with your aunt at Southsea for a week or two. You can get some sea air inside you and plenty of exercise and see what that will do. Once and for all I will not have that sulking."

One of the parts of the world that has not changed much in over thirty years is that wide stretch of river in the valley of the Ouse. Like much else, of course, it has changed a little. The house called Orleans, for example, has a different name. Whoever owns it calls it The Prospect now. They have also pollarded the limes, cut away the old mullein wilderness at the back and laid steep well-mown lawns that run right down to the huge balsam poplars by the riverside.

But on the whole it has not changed much. And in summer, now that I am almost as old as Miss Carfax, which of course is not really old as we think of age today, I like to go and look at it. I like to stand on the high road above the valley and stare down at the water lilies that are so much like white ducks, the crowds of little blue and amber butterflies that tremble about the grass seed and the lovers who lie kissing in the meadows, not caring if they are seen, on Sunday afternoons.

And as I do so I remember, always, the Queen of Spain Fritillary.